An Island Of My Own

An Island Of My Own

by
Andrea Spalding

A SANDCASTLE BOOK
A MEMBER OF THE DUNDURN GROUP
TORONTO

Editor: Joy Gugeler
Cover Illustrations: Janet Wilson
Production and Design: Teresa Bubela
Printer: Webcom

Library and Archives Canada Cataloguing in Publication

Spalding, Andrea
    An island of my own / by Andrea Spalding.

ISBN 978-1-55002-635-1

    I. Title.

PS8587.P213I84 2007   jC813'.54   C2007-901098-9

1   2   3   4   5   12   11   10   09   08

Conseil des Arts du Canada   Canada Council for the Arts

ONTARIO ARTS COUNCIL
CONSEIL DES ARTS DE L'ONTARIO

Canada

We acknowledge the support of the Canada Council for the Arts and the Ontario Arts Council for our publishing program. We also acknowledge the financial support of the Government of Canada through the Book Publishing Industry Development Program and The Association for the Export of Canadian Books, and the Government of Ontario through the Ontario Book Publishers Tax Credit program, and the Ontario Media Development Corporation.

Care has been taken to trace the ownership of copyright material used in this book. The author and the publisher welcome any information enabling them to rectify any references or credits in subsequent editions.

J. Kirk Howard, President

Printed and bound in Canada.
Printed on recycled paper.
www.dundurn.com

Dundurn Press	Gazelle Book Services Limited	Dundurn Press
3 Church Street, Suite 500	White Cross Mills	2250 Military Road
Toronto, Ontario, Canada	High Town, Lancaster, England	Tonawanda, NY
M5E 1M2	LA1 4XS	U.S.A. 14150

For Pat and Angela with love

Without whom we may never have
discovered small west coast islands

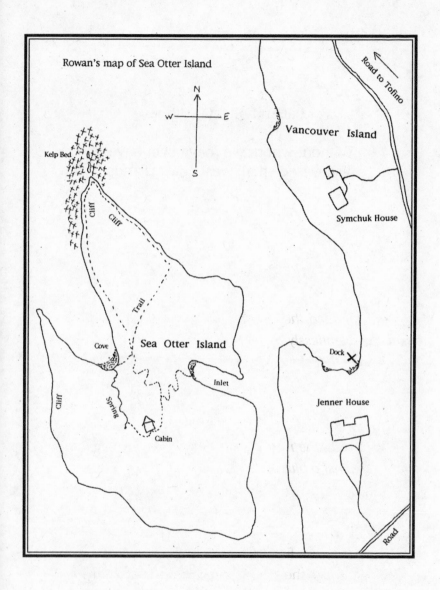

Rowan's map of Sea Otter Island

N
W — E
S

Kelp Bed

Cliff

Cliff

Trail

Cove

Cliff

Spring

Sea Otter Island

Inlet

Cabin

Vancouver Island

Road to Tofino

Symchuk House

Dock ✗

Jenner House

Road

Chapter One

The island lay quietly, swathed in veils of morning mist. The mist hid its colours, obscured the tops of the great cedar trees on its crown, draped the headland and rocky cliffs and muffled the sound of the long Pacific breakers pounding relentlessly along its western shore.

For years the island had waited, keeping its secret and dreams, but now the Girl had come and with her, change.

A small boat cut gently through the water, bringing the sound of laughter.

With a sigh, the mist parted, hung for a while in filmy ribbons against a blue sky, then dissolved.

On a wisp of breeze the island whispered. Would the Girl hear its voice?

Rowan was the first to hear them. Everyone else was pounding through the woods and calling to each other, but Rowan was standing quietly, leaning against a giant cedar. First she heard a high pitched whistle, then a distant splash.

"Hey, what's that noise?" Rowan asked. There was a

moment's peace while the others listened. Then, impatient to carry on exploring, the boys headed off again, pushing their way through the deer trail.

"I only hear Martin and Pat bushwhacking," laughed Darcy as she pounded through the undergrowth in their wake.

Rowan listened again. It took concentration to shut out her cousins' movements, the rustling tree branches, the unfamiliar bird calls, and the constant *shushing* of the nearby ocean.

There it was again. An unmistakable whistle. It came from her right. Rowan carefully parted the salal bushes and scrambled over fallen tree trunks. Suddenly the trees thinned and she could see she was not far from the edge of a cliff.

"Remember, cliffs may be undercut," echoed her uncle's warning. Rowan dropped to her hands and knees and edged slowly forward over the rocky ground. Gingerly she poked her head over the edge. It was a long way down to the ocean foaming on the rocky reef below.

Rowan's eyes scanned the cliff face. Good, no under-cutting, and the top wasn't crumbling at the edge. She relaxed. The tension slipped out of her and she felt her body melt into the ground as her skin absorbed the warmth of the sunshine on her back. The ocean heaved in restless oily swells and the sun glinted on a patch of shiny kelp heads bobbing up and down. Suddenly a ripple caught her eye. A dark bump appeared in the middle of the ripple. Then came a quick shaking movement and the sun sparkled on tiny drops of water fanning through the air before splattering into the surrounding sea.

"Sea otters," breathed Rowan in delight. "And there's another, and another. So that's what I heard." She cushioned her chin on her arms, made herself comfortable and watched with delight as the otter family swam, splashed and foraged in the green depths.

"Hey, Rowan! ROWAN! Where are you?" Martin's shrill voice cut through her concentration.

"Over here," Rowan called back. "I'm on the cliff edge though, so be careful." She listened as they came closer. "And try not to make too much noise, I've something to show you."

The cousins curiously, but not very quietly, broke through the trees.

"Great view. You can see two other islands from here," exclaimed Martin. He dropped down on the ground beside Rowan and peered over the cliff. "Have you found a way to get down the cliff? I could do it, but I might need a rope."

"Why climb here? It's a sheer drop to the water," said Pat.

"A climb's a climb." Martin looked over the cliff thoughtfully. "Yup. Bet I could do it."

"Oh shut up you two," said Rowan crossly. "If you can stay silent for a few minutes, I'll show you something. Just lie here and look out over the water, about ten metres from the shore. But be quiet."

The four cousins lay on their stomachs and hung over the cliff.

"Hey Pat, how far down can you spit?" whispered Martin.

"Oh for heaven's sake," muttered Darcy. "Rowan was trying to show us something."

The two boys flashed unrepentant grins at the older girls and turned back to scanning the ocean.

"What exactly are we looking for?" asked Pat politely.

Martin snickered.

Rowan shook her head, and gazed at the water. Suddenly she dug her elbow sharply into Darcy's ribs. "There, over to the left, beyond the rocks."

"Great... otters... at least three of them. Good for you, Rowan. We'll have to bring mom and dad up to see them," Darcy whispered enthusiastically.

"I love watching sea otters, they're so cute," remarked Rowan happily.

Darcy chuckled. "Well, you're out of luck. We don't have any."

"What do you mean?"

"Those are river otters. They live on land. They're quite common up and down the west coast. They spend lots of time in the ocean, so people often confuse them with sea otters."

Rowan looked unconvinced. "They look like sea otters to me."

Darcy shook her head. "Not a chance. The real sea otters are rare. There *are* some way up north, but not around here."

Darcy backed away from the cliff edge carefully, stood up and stretched. "Come on, let's show Rowan the cabin before we have to leave."

Martin and Patrick were off like a shot, slashing at the bushes.

Rowan hung back and looked out at the otters again. She was puzzled. She'd seen both sea otters and river otters before and could have sworn.... Oh well, Darcy was probably right. She was the one who lived here and knew the area. Rowan turned and pushed her way back through the salal bushes and onto the trail.

Martin and Patrick were leapfrogging over bushes and yelling creative insults at each other. Rowan winced and Darcy looked sympathetic.

"I know, they're a bit much. But they're OK, just noisy. Mom says it's 'third child syndrome' but because they're twins it's doubled." Darcy gave Rowan's arm a friendly squeeze. "You'll soon get used to us again, and we like having you. Besides, I need a 'sister' with this mob."

Rowan smiled and gratefully returned the older girl's squeeze. "I'd like to be sisterly, but I'm not very good at it. I never know what to say to the twins." She paused searching for the right words. "And Bevan acts so grown up these days, he makes me feel uncomfortable. It's like having another uncle."

"Naw, he just likes to think he's grown up. When he's not with his university friends he's just the same. Don't let him give you a hard time."

"I'll try not to," Rowan smiled.

Rowan had always enjoyed visiting her cousins, but she hadn't seen them for three years and a lot had changed. Bevan, who used to tease and wrestle with her, was now a handsome university student of nineteen. He didn't seem to want to be bothered with a fifteen-year-old cousin. As for the twins, they were two loud, noisy human bulldozers, totally self-absorbed and living in a world of their own.

"I wonder if I can fit in here for six months?" thought Rowan uneasily. It was a long time to be without her parents, and the days seemed to stretch ahead interminably. Thank goodness Darcy hasn't changed much, even though she is older.

Darcy still liked to whisper in bed at night and always included Rowan on outings with her friends. Unfortunately Rowan didn't know what to say to *them* either. Rowan's life had been so different.

Most of her fifteen years were spent travelling around the world while her parents completed assignments. They were environmental journalists who spent their life chasing stories. Instead of attending a Canadian school she worked on courses by correspondence so she didn't meet other students. Rowan felt at home in many countries and cities and could speak four different languages but she wasn't used to people her own age.

Darcy's voice broke into her thoughts. "Look, here's the spring." Darcy stooped, lifted aside some ferns and showed Rowan the tiny runnel of crystal water trickling and dripping over some moss-covered rocks. "The cabin's over to your left, on the other side of the alder thicket."

Rowan obediently pushed through the bushes.

The cabin was tiny but perfect. A cedar log building barely three metres square, stood in a sunny clearing surrounded by cedars, alders, and a graceful maple tree whose curving branches hovered protectively over its roof. The sunshine glinted golden on the windows and the door stood open invitingly.

Rowan was rooted to the spot. In her dreams she had built a tiny house where she could retreat when she was tired of travelling and living in anonymous rented apartments. She'd imagined a simple cabin... in a beautiful forest... and here it was.

"Drat! The brats got here first," said Darcy cheerfully. "I

bet they're going to try and ambush us. Pretend to be surprised when they leap down from the sleeping loft inside."

Rowan barely heard what Darcy was saying. She stepped into the clearing and hesitantly walked toward the cabin door. Her hand stroked the mellowed wood of the door frame. It was warm, solid and inviting.

The interior was just as the outside had promised, perfect for one person. Here was a well-designed miniature home with just enough room for its cupboard, a wooden chair and small table. There was even a bookcase made of planks under the window. She imagined a bright cushion on the chair, a jar of wild flowers on the table, and some of her favourite books on the shelves.

"What's the ladder on the wall for?" she asked Darcy.

Immediately a cacophony of ear-piercing yells broke the silence and two bodies hurtled down from the shadows of the ceiling.

"Invaders!" screamed Martin deafeningly as he landed beside Rowan, giving her the fright of her life.

Darcy staggered against the wall with her hands up and mock fear on her face. "We surrender, we surrender, but spare us, we're only the advance scouts. The main boarding party is just about to land on the southern beach."

Pat waved on his comrade. "Forward!" he ordered. "The battle is not yet won. Let a surprise attack be the order of the day." He and Martin sped out of the cabin, across the clearing, and into the trees.

Rowan gazed at Darcy in admiration. "How on earth did you think of that?"

Darcy grinned. "Long practice. If you play along they

don't bug you half as much. Watch Mom. She's really good at it." She paused, her hands at the base of the ladder. "Come and see the sleeping loft."

The two girls climbed the short ladder and edged themselves into the loft.

"Just a minute, let me fix the shutter," muttered Darcy, and she wriggled up to the far end and began fiddling with something. Suddenly there was a clatter, and light streamed into the loft area, making both girls blink.

"The twins closed it so we wouldn't see them," Darcy explained.

Rowan looked around with a soft smile. The loft was really no more than a big shelf open on one side to the cabin below, but it was dry and solid. Her imagination furnished it with a mattress topped with a brightly-coloured quilt and a small chest.

Darcy patted the heavy roof beams. "Mom and Dad built this well. It's still weatherproof even though it's not been used for ages."

"Aunt Anne and Uncle Grant built this? I thought this island didn't belong to them?"

"It doesn't," explained Darcy. "It belongs to old Mr. Symchuk, but people around here are very helpful. Years ago when Mom needed to get away from everything and concentrate on her painting, Mr. Symchuk lent her his island. She stayed here on and off for a couple of years and he didn't charge her any rent. In return, she and Dad built the cabin and they left it for Mr. Symchuk's use."

Rowan nodded and looked around with renewed interest. "So this is the island where Aunt Anne painted?"

Darcy nodded. "Yes, the nature paintings she did before

she married Dad were all painted here. Mom was only eighteen when she first lived here on her own. She loved the island."

Darcy looked at her watch. "We'd better head back to the beach. Dad said he'd bring the boat over and pick us up about five o'clock."

Rowan laughed. "So that's why the boys headed off to the beach so fast. There really was a landing party!"

Chuckling, the two girls closed up the little cabin and left it in peace. But for several nights Rowan's dreams were haunted by elusive images of otters playfully curving through green waves and a sunlit glade containing a tiny cedar cabin.

Rowan's Journal

Sat June 30th

Why did my parents do this to me? Stick me with this family for six months. I'm scared I'll never fit in.

I didn't realize how big Canada was. The west coast is thousands of miles away from the apartment we had in Toronto and my cousins live in the middle of nowhere. The nearest so-called 'town' is half an hour's drive. It's one street and doesn't even have a movie theatre.

It is beautiful here though. The beaches go on for ever and you can always hear the ocean.

The best thing so far was the visit to the island. It was really weird to find out the cabin I'd imagined is real. Now I can't get it out of my mind. It felt inviting, like real at home.

I desperately miss Mom and Dad. I'm scared for them. Rwanda is half a world away and the news about what is happening there is awful. I wish there was a way to phone them. Letters take too long.

Chapter Two

The island waited patiently, as it had waited for years. The night wind rustled the cedars, then swooped down in an eddy to stir the fern fronds growing around the cabin's foundation. An owl called, and the deer mouse crossing the clearing froze until the eerie echo died away, then it scampered to safety among the roots of the maple tree.

The Girl had visited, but had she understood?

The cedars shivered with the wind of change and the island gathered its forces to send a message.

The owl called again.

Rowan woke up with a start and looked across the room. Darcy lay tidily under her duvet. Rowan looked down at her own rumpled bed. She had tossed and turned so much that the sheet had come untucked at the bottom, and the duvet had slipped off to one side.

She slid quietly out of bed and tucked everything back in place, then padded across the floor and looked through the window. The moonlight dappled the trees and glinted on the distant water. The faint drumming of a passing ship's engine throbbed rhythmically, vibrating the still air.

The island is just out there," she thought. "And my dream cabin... I wish I was sleeping there. I wonder if the otters are still awake?" She rested her head against the cool window glass and let the soothing peace of the night wrap itself around her, unlike the jarring activities of the day.

Sunday had been disastrous. The twins had booby-trapped the breakfast cereal so when Rowan lifted up the packet everything had fallen out—Corn Flipflaps all over the place!

Next came the "accident." The twins were working on building a model antique biplane and it was ready to fly. As they figured out the remote control, it jammed. The plane crashed down on Rowan and caught in her hair. The propeller wound round and round and nearly pulled a hunk of hair out at the roots. Aunt Anne had to cut the plane free. Not only was Rowan's head tender, she sported a bald patch and looked and felt like a freak.

The third disaster was supper and was really her own fault. Bevan had been ignoring her so she decided to prove she wasn't a kid. She unpacked a simple black mini-dress and changed for supper.

"Did someone die?" asked Martin.

Bevan grinned lazily. "Which one are you trying to impress?" he asked, "Martin or Pat?"

The twins made gagging noises and everyone else cracked up.

Rowan's face flamed at the memory. She had to admit that a black mini-dress that was fine in a Toronto restaurant looked pretty silly at an informal meal where everyone else was in shorts and T-shirts.

Rowan sighed. The whirling memories made sleep seem further further away. She tiptoed carefully across the room, quietly opened the door and padded down stairs to the kitchen.

She filled the kettle, plugged it in, then looked for some hot chocolate mix in the cupboard. She and her parents always made a late night drink of hot chocolate before bed.

Thinking about her parents made Rowan's eyes grow misty and she could hardly see her cup.

She stood up quickly to place the dirty spoon in the sink, but her hand shook. The spoon slipped and fell on the tiles with a clatter that echoed through the silent house.

She stood frozen and listened, her eyes on the door. To her embarrassment she saw it slowly swing open. "If that's the twins," she thought, "I'll scream."

Aunt Anne drifted sleepily into the kitchen clutching an old terry robe around her. "Oh, it's you Rowan. Is everything alright?"

"Yes," replied Rowan. Then she sat down at the breakfast bar, put her head in her hands, and began to cry.

Aunt Anne hugged her sleepily. "It's OK Rowan. You were bound to get homesick sooner or later."

Rowan dashed the tears angrily from her eyes. "How can I be homesick... I don't have a home... I just miss people ... I'll never fit in here... everyone thinks I'm a freak."

"No one thinks you are a freak Rowan, but your lifestyle is so different from ours that you are bound to have some trouble adjusting."

"No one understands anything I say," cried Rowan. "When I said my parents were on the Zaire-Rwanda border doing a story on the mountain gorillas, Darcy's friends said 'Oh. That's nice,' as though my parents were on holiday. Then they carried on talking about the latest film they'd seen."

She thumped the table in frustration. "It's not 'nice', it's horrible....They're in a war zone... in the place where Diane Fossey got killed for trying to protect the gorillas... but it's an important story to do... I... I just wish I could talk to them sometimes."

By this time the tears were pouring unchecked down Rowan's face. "My parents are risking their life for a story. An', an', no-one here cares," she hiccupped.

Aunt Anne drew Rowan close and rocked her as she sobbed.

"We care, Rowan. We love your parents too. We worry about them all the time. But don't blame the kids around here. You have to be fair to them."

Rowan pulled away and looked at her aunt.

"It's not that they don't care," continued Anne, "it's just that *you* know more than they do. You know what the story is because you heard your parents talk about their research. You have information the other kids don't. Darcy's friends won't understand until your parent's story is published in a newspaper or magazine, and they can read it."

Anne patted Rowan's shoulder and found a tissue for her.

Rowan blew her nose and looked watery-eyed at her aunt. "Aunt Anne?"

Anne looked at her serious face.

"Yes Rowan?"

"What if... I mean... " There was a pause while she took a deep breath and tried to collect herself. She spoke the next words very slowly and clearly "What—happens—if—my—parents—never—finish the story? What happens if they are killed?"

Anne cradled Rowan close. "That won't happen. Your parents are careful and experienced and don't take chances. But if something *does* happen, then you have a home with us... I know you're worried... me too... I guess that's why both of us have trouble sleeping."

Rowan nodded miserably.

Aunt Anne hugged her even tighter. "Every night we have to be as brave and as sensible as your parents." She looked Rowan firmly in the eye. "Your parents knew that if they found themselves in a tight spot, they would have to move fast." She gave Rowan a squeeze. "They couldn't worry about you as well. See? Staying here makes them safer."

Rowan gave a tremulous smile of relief. "I hadn't thought of it that way. I just felt guilty because I was safe and they weren't."

"Well, now you can relax" said Anne briskly. "Come on. Time for bed. Try and think of something you can do here, instead of worrying about Mom and Dad."

Rowan said good night and went back upstairs. Her head turning over a new idea. Using her flashlight so she wouldn't wake Darcy, she quickly scribbled in her journal.

Sunday June 31st
Midnight

> *I can't be with Mom and Dad, but talking with Anne gave me an idea. I can research an environmental story just like they do. Something to share with them when they come home.*
>
> *I've thought and thought about it, and I don't think the otters I saw on the island were river otters. I think they were sea otters. They are like the ones Mom and I watched down in California in Monterey Bay.*
>
> *No one here believes me, so I am going to have to prove it.*
>
> *First I have to see if I can spend time on the island, in the cabin, like Aunt Anne did when she was painting.*
>
> *I want to observe, and take notes and photos and do some research.*
>
> *If they really are sea otters, I will be on to a big story.*

Rowan closed her journal, then slid it under her pillow.

The veils of mists gathered protectively around the island, and sent filmy fingers drifting across the channel. They drifted through Rowan's window and closed around her sleeping form cocooning her in a web of dreams. She smiled in her sleep.

Chapter Three

Monday was a holiday. Rowan awoke with the robins. She laughed as she drew back the bedroom curtains and saw one, his chest puffed out importantly, singing noisily under the nearby dogwood tree.

She turned back to the bedroom and looked at the hump under the adjacent bed. "Hey, come on Darcy. Wake up. It's a beautiful day and I've got an idea."

Darcy muttered unintelligibly and turned over.

Rowan leaned over and shook her. "Darcy! Wake up. I need to talk to you."

Darcy sat up uncertainly. Her hair hung over her face and her eyes were bleary with sleep. "Is something wrong?" she asked. She ran her finger through her mop and tried to focus on her cousin.

Rowan laughed. "No, nothing's wrong. Things are right for a change. Listen Darcy... I know what I want to do." She sat back and waited eagerly for Darcy's reply.

Darcy looked uncomprehendingly at Rowan. Then she stretched out an arm and fumbled around on the bedside table until her fingers found the alarm clock. She lifted it slowly in front of her face and focussed carefully on the dial for a few moments.

"Rowan, it's not even seven. You're waking me up to tell me about what? Some hair-brained scheme? Thanks a lot!" Darcy pulled the sheet over her head and plumped back down on her pillow.

"Aw, come on Darcy," wheedled Rowan, "I'm bursting to tell someone."

"Find the twins," said the unsympathetic bump under the bed sheets. "They're always up early."

Even that couldn't dampen Rowan's mood. She clattered cheerfully down the stairs and into the kitchen. A warm and fragrant smell hung in the air. "Mmmm," she said appreciatively. "Do I smell waffles?"

Uncle Grant and the twins looked up in surprise. Her uncle was skillfully flipping a steaming waffle onto Pat's plate while Martin was wielding the syrup jug over one he had already half demolished.

"Oh oh, sleeping beauty's awake," snickered Martin.

"Maybe she thinks there's a handsome prince around," Pat joined in the teasing.

But this morning Rowan was equal to anything. "That's right," she agreed. "But I only see toads." She advanced towards the boys. "Do I have to kiss them?"

With a loud "YUCK" both boys grabbed their plates and forks and vanished through the patio doors.

There was the sound of gentle applause. Rowan turned to see her uncle and aunt smiling and clapping their hands.

"Congratulations, Rowan. You're learning to handle the twins!" Grant gestured towards the waffle iron. "As a reward you get the next waffle. Find yourself a plate and some cutlery."

Rowan sat hungrily at the breakfast bar. "Great. I'm starving," she said with a grin. "I hope I'm not taking your breakfast."

Anne laughed and came to sit beside her. "There's plenty for everyone," she said. "Why are you so bright-eyed and bushy-tailed this morning?"

Rowan grinned. "I guess 'cause I unloaded on you last night."

Uncle Grant smiled and ruffled her hair as he placed a waffle-laden plate in front of her.

"You made me think about things differently," Rowan continued. "So I got an idea."

Grant gave a loud sigh of mock despair and waved his hands in the air. "I might have known. All the crazy schemes in this family seem to start with ideas from my wife. Well? Come on. Out with it!"

Rowan moved to the fridge and poured herself a glass of milk. "It's like this," she explained between gulps. "Because my family travel around the world, I've done most of my schooling by correspondence."

Anne and Grant nodded.

"Some of the courses were pretty boring," she explained, "so Dad developed a special way of making my education more fun."

Grant grinned. "That sounds like David, alright," he agreed.

"So," continued Rowan, "every time we were in a place for a few weeks, I did a special project that had to do with where we were living. See, Dad thinks there is no point in travelling unless you understand something about the place you are visiting."

"I remember," interjected Anne. "The last time you came to stay with us you were interested in totem poles."

Rowan nodded enthusiastically. "That's right. I learned to recognize the carved symbols, like the design for the salmon, and the raven, and the eagle. I got so I could 'read' totem poles. I still remember how to do it."

"OK, OK, we're with you," Grant said. "So you've thought of a project for this visit?"

"Yup. I want to go and live on Mr. Symchuck's island, on my own, like Anne did, only just for a couple of weeks. Then I can learn something about the birds and the animals there, especially the otters. I want to observe them and photograph them and record what I see." She stopped and looked at them both. "Please, please say yes?"

There was a long pause as Grant and Anne looked at each other.

"Have you ever done any camping?" asked Anne slowly.

Rowan nodded her head. "Of course. We weren't always in cities, you know. I've camped in the desert. But anyway, it wouldn't be real camping. There's the cabin. It's not like a tent that could get flooded out or blown down."

"What about cooking. What would you do for food?" asked Grant, serving Anne another waffle.

"I can cook," said Rowan indignantly. "I've been cooking for years."

"But it's a bit different when there's no running water, only a little camp stove and no fridge," Grant insisted.

"I know where the spring is. And I've helped Mom and

Dad make meals on the camp stove when we've been travelling together. You could show me how your camp stove works," insisted Rowan. "And we've stayed in lots of places were there were no fridges and we had to be very careful about what we ate and how we prepared food."

Rowan grinned across at her aunt and uncle. "I might dress for dinner, but I'm not a wimp you know."

She started ticking items off on her fingers. "I'd have to pack clothes, organize and plan my food, prepare the pit toilet. I know not to light fires in the bush, and we'd have to figure out a method of checking in with each other." She paused and looked challengingly across at her aunt and uncle. "You did it Aunt Anne, and you were barely older than I am! Besides there is nothing on the island that could harm me!"

"That's certainly true." Anne stood up and stretched. "Look Rowan, leave it with us for a while. We need to think things over. Can we talk later this evening?"

Rowan nodded. "I guess that's fair." She stood up happily. "Well at least you haven't said 'No' yet."

"OK," said Grant and Anne. "But don't get your hopes up. You need more than our permission. We'd have to discuss this with Mr. Symchuck too."

Rowan threw a wicked glance at her aunt and uncle. "Well, you managed that kind of request successfully when you wanted to live there for a couple of years. I guess you should have no trouble asking about a couple of weeks."

"Don't push your luck!" Grant said waving a waffle-tipped fork threateningly.

Rowan laughed and skipped quickly out of the kitchen, already beginning to make plans.

The island spread its beauties in the sunshine and sighed with relief.

Chapter Four

The meeting with Anne and Grant was set for seven, but by six that evening a separate discussion was being held in the family room. Darcy and the twins were determined to help Rowan get to the island.

"Let's list everything you need," said Darcy and she and Rowan sprawled on the floor alternately chewing their pencils and scribbling notes.

"It's a brilliant project," said Pat enthusiastically.

"Yup," agreed Martin. "But you need us along to protect you."

"I don't need protection," protested Rowan. "No one ever goes to the island. It's not very big, and because it's close to shore it's not considered a challenge like the distant islands. Besides, I want to do this on my own."

"You may live to regret it," warned Martin in his most dramatic voice.

"Never mind, we'll have to go over with her anyway, Martin," comforted Pat.

"You will?" interjected Rowan and Darcy together.

"Why?"

"To set up a radio communication system and surveillance," explained Pat.

"Yeah, and booby traps to catch anyone who *does* land there," agreed Martin.

"Forget it," said Rowan rudely as she and Darcy rolled their eyes.

"Hello. Do I hear plotting?" a new voice broke onto the scene.

Everyone's head swivelled sharply.

"Hi, Bevan," said Rowan shyly, but her greeting was lost in the yells of welcome as the twins threw themselves on their older brother.

"Lay off, brats," said Bevan calmly stretching out his arms and easily holding each twin at arm's length. "You'll embarrass my guest."

The twins stopped wrestling and peered around Bevan's bulk. A slight Chinese student stepped forward, smiled at them and bowed his head politely towards the girls.

"Hey, are you Hoy Chan?" asked Pat eagerly. "Bevan's friend from Hong Kong who knows six different Chinese dialects?"

"Yes, that's correct," said Hoy with a grin. "A skill that has limited use in Canada."

"What do you mean? It's great," burbled Pat enthusiastically as he shook off Bevan's restraining hand. "We've been wanting to meet you." Pat bounced over and pumped Hoy's hand. "I'm Pat and this is Martin."

"Yeah, really pleased to meet you." Martin, too, disengaged himself from Bevan and grinned at Hoy.

"Can you teach us Chinese? Then we can write or speak to each other and no one else will be able to understand us."

Hoy chuckled, a surprisingly deep and infectious laugh that shook his slight frame. Rowan, watching him with interest, found herself grinning in response.

"Unfortunately to learn even one of the Chinese dialects would take longer than my visit," Hoy explained courteously to the boys. "However if we could arrange to meet tomorrow morning for half an hour, I will show you several symbols that you could use as a code."

"Right on!" exclaimed Martin. "How about eight, right after breakfast?"

"Hold it." Bevan placed a warning hand on each of the twins shoulders. "Hoy is our guest. He might not want to get up that early. How about ten instead."

"Ten!" chorused two disgusted voices. "That's nearly afternoon."

"If I may interrupt," broke in Hoy, "could we compromise by meeting at nine. I am sure to be wide awake by then."

"Right. That's settled. Now let me introduce you to the rest of the tribe." Bevan gestured towards the two girls. "My sister Darcy." Darcy sat up and pushed the hair out of her eyes and waved. "And our cousin Rowan Feldman."

Rowan clambered to her feet, walked over and shook Hoy's hand. "*Nai ho ma*," she said shyly.

The younger members of the family stared at her with their mouths open, and Bevan's eyebrows shot up to his hairline.

"Was that Chinese?" whispered Martin to Pat. "Does Rowan know Chinese? What's she saying?"

Rowan turned smiling to the group. "I was just saying

'Hello, How are you.' Remember, we lived in Hong Kong for two years? I learned a bit of Chinese there." She turned again to Hoy. "I have difficulty writing though. There are so many characters to remember."

Hoy bowed. "Thank you for trying. Many westerners find it a troublesome language."

Rowan flushed with pleasure.

Bevan gave Rowan a friendly pat on the shoulder. "You are full of surprises. And what's all this I hear about you wanting to head out to Mr. Symchuk's island?"

"Have you been talking to Mom and Dad?" demanded Darcy. "What did they say? Are they going to let her?"

Bevan laughed. "I'm not telling. You'll have to ask them."

"That's it, you can go," squealed Darcy and she and the twins jumped up and down and slapped Rowan on the back excitedly.

Rowan extracted herself with difficulty. "How do you know?" she asked, mystified.

"Because Bevan was laughing and wouldn't tell us," Darcy explained.

Rowan still looked uncertain.

"It's true. You'll see," corroborated Martin. "If they weren't going to let you, Bevan would have looked serious and told us not to bank on it."

Bevan and Hoy burst out laughing.

"I see this family knows each other too well," remarked Hoy.

"Judging from the racket, I'd say someone's let the cat out of the bag." Anne and Grant had entered the room unnoticed.

Rowan swung round. "Is it true? Are you really going to

let me go to the island?" she demanded eagerly.

They nodded, but Anne held up her hand for silence to prevent another outburst.

"Rowan, you have Mr. Symchuk's permission to stay there for two or three weeks if you wish, on one condition."

"OK. What's the condition?" asked Rowan eagerly.

"That you do absolutely nothing to damage or alter the island. Mr. Symchuk is about to put it up for sale and wants it left in pristine condition."

There was dead silence.

"Mr. Symchuk wants to *sell* the island?" said Darcy in disbelief. "But I thought he loved it?"

"He does," Anne agreed. "But he's an old man and can't get out there easily, and he needs the money."

"Hey Dad! Why don't we buy it?" suggested Pat eagerly.

Grant shook his head. "Sorry son. We don't have that kind of cash."

"But if Mr. Symchuk sells it we might not be able to go there again. The new owners might not let us," Martin protested. "And we've always gone there."

"I know," said Anne briskly. "But these things happen. Mr. Symchuk has been very generous allowing us to use it when we wanted. You'll just have to make the best of it this summer." She looked across at Rowan. "Well my dear, still raring to go?"

"You bet," Rowan replied eagerly. "Of course I'll look after the island."

"Then you and I and Grant need to sit down together and make a plan," suggested Anne. "In the meantime, why don't Martin and Pat gather the camping supplies, the stove, water containers and cooking supplies."

"It's OK Mom, we know what's needed," Pat assured her. "Come on Martin, lets go!"

"I'll find the sleeping bag, foam mattress, and towels and things," offered Darcy.

"If you don't mind, Hoy and I will make ourselves scarce, but we'll help you load the boat tomorrow," Bevan offered.

"Thanks Bevan, Hoy, that's much appreciated." Grant turned to Rowan. "Now young woman. Why don't we go through your list and make sure nothing is missing."

It took several hours to get things organized, but by the time Rowan went to bed that night she was ready.

Rowan's Journal

Monday July 1st

> *They're letting me go!!!!!*
> *I can hardly believe it. Two whole weeks in a tiny cabin on an island of my own.*
> *I'll ask Bevan to drive me into Tofino in the morning to pick up a notebook and some more film for my camera. Dad said a good camera was important. He'll be thrilled if I use it for the sea otter project.*

From across the channel, the distant call of an owl wobbled through the midnight air. Rowan lifted her head, and strained her ears, but the call came only once.

Chapter Five

It was afternoon before Rowan's supplies were ready to be packed aboard the family's powerboat, *Nootka*.

"Am I really going to need all that... just for two weeks?" asked Rowan in amazement as she surveyed the pile of boxes on the dock.

Anne laughed. "I know, I felt the same way. But you can bet no matter how much stuff you take, you will discover something vital has been forgotten."

Rowan shook her head in disbelief. "We must have everything but the kitchen sink."

Anne clapped her hand to her forehead. "That's it! I knew we were missing something. You need the pail for hauling water and a bowl for washing. See... the kitchen sink!"

Eventually, no one could think of any other item, and the essentials had been checked and rechecked. Everything was safely loaded, the ropes cast off and *Nootka* puttered quietly away from the dock, towing a small dinghy.

Ten minutes later they were out of the sheltered bay,

bouncing across the narrow channel separating the island from the mainland, then nosing into the tiny inlet that served as a landing area.

Rowan felt distinctly territorial as they dropped anchor and pulled the little dinghy they had been trailing, alongside *Nootka*.

"All hands on deck," called Anne. "Time to unload."

Rowan crossed her fingers hoping she could go first, for it would take several trips to ferry the supplies to the beach.

"Pat, Martin, and Rowan, you go now. Pat can row out and land on the beach with Rowan. Martin, when everything's unloaded, you row the dinghy back for the next load."

Rowan sighed with relief.

Pat grinned at her as she stepped gingerly into the dinghy, paused to get her balance, then clumsily took the boxes he handed down to her. "It's OK, Rowan, we all know you want to land first."

"Yeah, in fact you can do the unpacking yourself if you'd rather!" teased Martin.

"Looking for an excuse to get out of work?" asked Rowan.

The two boys grinned cheekily and swung down into the little dinghy. Martin slid past the boxes with the ease of long practice and Pat grasped the oars.

Rowan perched in the prow, leaning forward like a figurehead in her eagerness to reach the beach.

Only the faintest remnants of mist still drifted around the island shores; the rest had burnt off in brilliant sunshine.

The island was in celebration, decked out gloriously in welcome. The grasses on the headland, starred with a thousand flowers, rippled and danced, and the ferns fringing the forest nodded and swayed. Around the rocks the ocean frothed with creamy lace and the waves beneath Rowan's little boat sparkled and shone as they carried her gently forward.

The keel of the boat scraped the bottom. Pat competently shipped the oars, and he and Martin leapt out and dragged the boat further up the shore. Then they promptly pulled two kazoos out of their pockets and played a rousing chorus of "Oh Canada." Pat bowed low to Rowan and offered her his hand to step from the boat. Rowan giggled and stepped over the bow in an elegant fashion. Martin stuck out his foot and tripped her.

Rowan sprawled across the wet sand as Pat, in the rounded tones of the late-night news announcer gave a vivid description of Lady Rowan bending down to kiss the ground and claim this new country for Canada.

Rowan sat up to the sound of cheers from *Nootka*. She grinned, brushed the sand off her face and waved regally.

"I should have known you would be up to something," she remarked to Pat and Martin. "But you wait, I'll get you yet."

"Oooh, we're really scared," Pat retorted cheekily.

It took four trips in the dinghy to unload the people and the supplies. Then everyone helped backpack them up the trail to the cabin.

"Mom, how many trips did you make when you and Dad carried your supplies?" asked Bevan as he stopped halfway to take a few deep breaths.

Anne laughed. "It wasn't the supplies that were the problem," she explained, "it was the logs we used to build the cabin. They were incredibly heavy."

Rowan listened to the conversation and felt guilty. She hadn't realized how much work her request to live on the island would make for everyone. The whole family had taken the day off to help her set up.

"Don't worry about it. We're all having a wonderful time," said Grant with a grin when she mentioned it to him. "Besides, it gets you out of our hair for a while!"

Rowan grinned back, shouldered her pack, and set off up the hill again.

By the middle of the afternoon, the cabin glade looked as if a tornado had struck. Boxes were scattered around in various stages of disarray. People rushed in and out of the cabin asking Rowan where she wanted things placed, and Grant and Anne were trying to give her instructions.

"Now you understand how to use the stove?"

Rowan nodded.

"Keep your perishables in the cool chest and eat them first."

Rowan nodded again.

"What are you going to do in a case of emergency?"

"I've got emergency flares, and someone will check on me once a day."

"Don't worry about emergencies, this radio should be working soon," called Martin.

Rowan looked unconvinced. Martin and Pat's effort to rig a short-wave radio involved aerial manouvres in trees, and metres of cable. It seemed unlikely to work.

Bevan winked at Grant, walked over to Rowan, casually slung his arm over her shoulder and steered her behind the cabin and out of sight of the twins.

Hoy was waiting. "Don't say anything to Martin and Pat," he whispered. "But I have something that might help." He handed Rowan a small box.

She lifted the lid and chuckled. "A cell phone!"

"My father's in electronics," explained Hoy. "He's loaned them. Bevan also has one, but we'll not spoil the twins' radio, eh?"

"Jeez... fantastic. Thanks Hoy."

"All the instructions are inside, with some spare batteries. We will call you later tonight to be sure everything is working."

By early evening everything was stowed and the boxes stored under a tarpaulin at the side of the cabin, ready for the trip back. Rowan, though thankful for all the help, was ready to be left alone. She wanted to feel the cabin and island were truly hers.

Anne gave her a bear hug.

"We'll leave now. We have to get back before the light goes. Still sure you want to stay all on your own?"

Rowan nodded and grinned. "I wouldn't dare say no after all this effort."

Anne patted her shoulder. "But you don't have to stay if you find it's too lonely."

"She won't be lonely for long," Martin chimed in. "We're coming over with Dad tomorrow to finish fixing up the radio."

Rowan rolled her eyes.

"Actually, I'd be rather relieved if you did have a working

radio, Rowan," said Anne worriedly. "I still wonder if I am doing the right thing letting you stay here on your own."

"Anne, stop worrying. She'll be fine," said Grant.

"I will, I will," Rowan agreed. "I spend a lot of time on my own normally." She grinned slyly at Hoy and Bevan. "I've everything I need and we've set up an emergency plan. What can possibly go wrong?"

"OK," Anne sighed. "I guess it will have to do. Come on Grant. Let's round everyone up and leave Rowan to enjoy her first night alone."

Rowan walked with them down the trail and watched from the beach. Eventually, they were all aboard and *Nootka* puttered slowly away. Rowan's final glimpse was of Anne waving madly from the deck as *Nootka* finally disappeared around the end of the inlet.

Rowan heaved a sigh of relief and turned to look at her island. The empty beach spread temptingly before her. "Yahoo!" she yelled and turned a couple of cartwheels.

"I'm alone... alone and in charge of myself for the first time in a month," Rowan thought as she ran eagerly up the trail to the cabin.

The little glade seemed larger now that everyone had left. Rowan wandered around looking with new eyes at the maple tree, the alder thickets, the salal bushes and towering cedars. She bent down and picked a few wild flowers and some interesting grasses and took them into the cabin. Rummaging in the cupboard she found a plastic glass, filled it with water from the container and set them in the middle of the table. Next she organized her books on the bookshelf, climbed the ladder, plumped up her sleeping bag and pillow and laid the spare blanket across the bottom. She sat back on her heels and surveyed everything.

It already looked like home. The water canister stood on the bench by the cupboard. The cupboard itself was organized into a food shelf and a shelf for the cooking implements. The basin stood beside the water container and the pail on the floor beneath the bench, along with a packet of garbage bags.

The table looked inviting with the flowers in the middle and the chair beside it, and through the open door Rowan could see the large flat stump in the glade, where Uncle Grant had set up her Coleman stove for cooking. The red propane tank gleamed, and so did the red fire extinguisher beside it.

Rowan sat cross-legged on her bed and unpacked her backpack. First she took out her camera, next the new spiral notebook and the pen she'd tied to the spine with a piece of string so as not to lose it. She laid them carefully beside her on the bed.

Rowan had already placed her suitcase full of clothes beside her bed to double as a night table. She pulled a flashlight out of her pack and placed it on top. Next she pulled out a photo of her parents and stood it up. Finally, from the bottom of the backpack, Rowan pulled a gossamer shawl from India. It was deep red, interwoven with silver threads. The threads, twinkled and sparkled where the light caught them. She climbed down the ladder and draped the beautiful piece of fabric over the back of the chair and stood back to admire the effect.

BRRRING, BRRRING. The piercing sound of the cell phone made her jump. She grabbed it off the table and fumbled to flip it open. "Hello?"

There was a crackle of static, but no voice.

"Hello.... Hello?" Rowan looked at the phone to see if she should have pushed anything else.

The static got worse then stopped. She realized the display at the top had a message—"Out of Area." She smiled and shrugged, laid the phone down and walked over to the doorway to survey her domain. The dusk had closed in and the evening insects were out in full force. She yawned. "Time to visit the outhouse then roll into bed early," she decided.

Cozily snuggled in her sleeping bag, Rowan lay on her stomach and wrote an account of the day in her journal. She could hear the breeze in the trees and the rustle of unidentified small animals in the undergrowth. A moth fluttered against the window, attracted by a light that wasn't usually there. In the background was the constant shushing of the ocean.

"What a nice way to be lulled to sleep," she thought as her eyes closed.

The moonlight filtered through the trees and the nightly mist swathed the island, hiding it protectively. All was well, the Girl was here. Nothing must disturb her slumber. The owl watched silently.

While Rowan was sleeping, the west coast phone lines were incredibly busy.

In the Jenner's household Hoy called his father in

Vancouver.

"Dad?"

"Yes Hoy."

"We need some help. You were right, the cell phones won't work in this area. Do you have any other equipment that might?"

"I'll see what I can do. I'm flying out to Tofino tomorrow, so I'll sort something out and bring it with me."

"Thanks, that's great. Are you still looking for real estate?"

"Yes. Heard of any?"

Hoy laughed. "Only an island!"

Also in Vancouver, but oblivious to Rowan and her island, wildlife biologist Katrina Vasey sat in front of her computer trying to contain a growing bubble of excitement.

It was late at night, but she wanted to finish entering the information that had come across by e-mail that day.

She checked the latest report, entered the coordinates, then waited for the result.

"Yes, approximately the same area!"

She leaned back, speaking out loud, with a broad grin on her face.

"It's time to organize a field trip to the west coast and check things out." She paused thoughtfully. "I'll do it on my own, then I won't be wasting much money if it's a false alarm."

She patted the computer. "But I've a feeling it's not. Three totally different reports from the same stretch of coastline. It's gotta be true." She looked at the time and pulled the phone towards her.

"Hello, is it Tofino Boat Rentals?"

"Yes, Tammy speaking. How can we help you?"

"Hi Tammy, it's Katrina Vasey. I'm the wildlife biologist who came out last year to do a survey on sea mammals."

"Why, hello Katrina. I didn't recognize your voice. Are you coming out again?"

"Yes, do you have a boat if I head out in the next couple of days?"

"Sure do. How big?"

"A small powerboat's fine, but something with a cabin so I can live aboard."

"OK, it'll be ready."

Katrina hung up, dialed another number, and left a message.

"Hello sir. This is Katrina. I thought I'd better let you know I won't be in the office tomorrow. In fact probably not for a few days. That sea otter lead I'm following up looks more and more likely. I've had three definite reports and a whole list of rumoured sightings. I've pinned it down to within a seven kilometre stretch of coast south of Long Beach, so I've hired a boat and I'm going out to check the likely kelp beds. I'll keep you posted."

Back on Vancouver Island's west coast, Mr. Symchuk looked thoughtfully at the phone and picked up the receiver.

Many kilometres away in the city of Nanaimo, the phone rang.

"Hello, Susan Symchuk here."

"It's me, sweetheart. How's Jaimie?"

"Not so good Dad. Julie's avoiding him and I don't know how much longer he'll respond to me."

"I want to ask you something, but I don't want you to feel I'm interfering."

"Dad, you've never done that."

"Well, I've heard of a very special treatment for Jaimie. But it's a school in the States. If I said it would be possible for you all to go, would you think about it?"

"Well, yes. But Dad, where would we get the money?"

"Don't worry, it will be available if you need it. I've put the island up for sale."

There was a long pause.

"Oh Dad," said Susan Symchuk with a sob in her voice. "You shouldn't have done that. But, thanks."

Chapter Six

Rowan woke with a start. Someone was on the roof. She could hear big boots scraping on the shingle shakes above her head. Terrified, Rowan slithered out of her sleeping bag, crept down the ladder, tiptoed to the doorway and opened it silently. Nothing in sight. She grabbed the emergency flare, held it at the ready, then erupted out of the cabin waving it frantically.

"Hey, who's there? Don't you know this is private property?" she called fiercely, but with a distinct note of panic in her voice.

Two large ravens flew off the cabin roof, perched on the nearest branch and glared at her.

Rowan giggled nervously and felt rather silly. She should have realized it couldn't be a person on the roof. But how was she to know ravens had such big feet?

The ravens spread their wings disdainfully and flapped lazily out of the clearing.

The adrenalin faded and Rowan replaced the flare in the cabin and sat down.

It was a wonderful morning. Though the hour was early the sky was already a hazy blue, the air warm, and wafts of steam rose mistily from the grass. The interior of the cabin seemed gloomy after the outside brightness though the hour was still, so Rowan lifted the table into the glade, placed the chair beside it and decided to enjoy her breakfast in the sunshine.

She went inside and rummaged through the cooler, gathered a slice of bread, some cheese, an apple and some fresh milk, and went outside again.

The air was full of sounds. Dozens of birds were singing and she could hear a woodpecker drumming on a tree. Rowan chuckled, the silence of the wild was a myth. She had never heard so much noise. A rustling and shaking caught her eye. Halfway up a big tree trunk a piece of bark was shaking and jiggling noisily. She froze and watched. The shaking continued for some time. Then she caught sight of a chickadee causing the noise. He was tiny, but he pulled and tugged at a piece of bark ten times larger than himself, to reach the insects hiding underneath.

"Here, try some cheese, little chickadee." She threw a corner across the glade within his reach. He fluttered away in fright.

An iridescent green hummingbird shot across the clearing and hovered hopefully in front of the red fuel tank of the Coleman stove. Her wings moved so fast they were a blur. As soon as Rowan shifted her body to get a closer look, the tiny bird vanished.

Crunching her apple, she moved around the clearing looking at everything with new eyes: the banana slug edging its way over the grass, the bracket fungus growing on a rotting stump, the delicate webbing of a dew-spangled spider web hanging between two branches, and the scurry of some unspecified tiny furry creature disappearing into the undergrowth. Everything was different now she was here on her own. All these things were part of her world and she was part of theirs.

The day stretched before her with no one to tell her what to do or where to go. The sense of freedom was almost frightening.

She took the pail to the spring and waited while the water trickled gently in. Here among the trees the light was a gentle green but the monotonous buzz of mosquitoes made her waft and slap at her arms and face to try and stop them biting.

"Drat," she muttered as she rubbed a particularly vicious bump. "I'll itch for days."

Washing herself, her plate and mug, and brushing her teeth didn't take long. She then turned her attention to the cabin, shook out her bedroll and pillow, and swept the floor.

Eagerly she grabbed her pack, slipped in her notebook, pen and camera, then a beach towel, novel, her wildlife identification book and a couple of cookies for good measure. Slinging her binoculars around her neck, Rowan closed the cabin door and headed down the deer trail to the cliff.

The ocean was as smooth as glass. Hardly a ruffle of wind disturbed its surface and there wasn't any sea life to be seen, only the glistening bobbing heads of the kelp. Rowan was incredibly disappointed. Somehow she'd expected the otters to be there waiting for her. Still she had all day if necessary, so she sat on a convenient tree stump and enjoyed the view.

Three bald eagles soared above her. One, a yearling, squawked intermittently. Below, way beyond her island, several small fishing vessels lazily puttered up the coast. Nearer, a small sailboat drifted, its sails hanging slackly in the still air, and she could see people sunbathing on its deck.

Suddenly the peace was rudely shattered. A sleek expensive power boat came screaming around the island in a shower of spray then coasted to a stop at the bottom of her cliff. Rowan could see several people using binoculars to rake the shore as they passed. Now they were looking at the cliff face.

Instinctively Rowan shrank back from the edge and hid behind the trunk of a tree. Safe in the shadows, she used her own binoculars to see what was going on. Something about those people made her wary. The boat was too sleek and its occupants too well-dressed to be nature lovers watching for seals, otters or birds. Besides, they were looking at a large sheet of paper spread over the boat's cabin roof and then pointing to different parts of the cliff.

"I bet that boat's been here earlier and that's why the otters aren't around," she thought.

Snatches of conversation drifted up over the water towards her.

"Almost thirty acres, well worth the asking price."

So that was it. These were real estate people viewing the island with an eye to selling it.

Rowan frowned. "I hope you don't find anyone to buy

Otter Island," she muttered, as she faded through the trees then walked quickly down the cliff trail to the cove on the other side of the headland.

The relief of finding the cove unoccupied swept over Rowan in a wave. No boats, friendly or unfriendly, disturbed the long Pacific swell as it undulated down toward the beach. She spread her arms and deeply breathed in freedom.

Walking slowly along the beach, Rowan checked the mounds of seaweed along the tideline for interesting flotsam, hoping against hope to find a Japanese glass fishing float. There was nothing other than a long piece of yellow nylon rope. She pulled it out, coiled it up for further use, and hooked it over a branch. The firm sand stretched out invitingly so she skipped and ran, making circles and swirls but pausing at intervals to pick up sand dollars scattered along the surface like stars.

Eventually she spread her towel and settled down against a comfortable log to read her book. It was so peaceful, just trees rustling, birdsong and the delightful shushing of the waves as they rushed up the beach towards her.

Rowan woke feeling uncomfortable. The sun was beating in her face, sweat trickled down her neck, and her backrest had developed a prominent spike that was digging into her back. She stretched stiffly, stood up and looked out across the water. A flash caught her eye. There seemed to be something splashing out by the kelp bed near the entrance to the cove.

Rowan mentally crossed her fingers, grabbed her binoculars and pack and headed up the headland path to watch.

It was the otters. Full of wonder, Rowan lay on her stomach high above the kelp bed, pulled out her notebook and carefully wrote down what she saw.

Wednesday 3rd July

> *Five otters in the kelp bed.*
> *Lots of activity. Otters swimming up to the surface of the water and back down under the shiny brown kelp. They seem to be feeding. Their mouths are constantly in motion, chewing fish and clams.*

Rowan grinned. She could hear the crunch of the clamshells from where she was sitting. What voracious eaters they were! She studied the heads that poked out of the water and continued her notes.

Suddenly, Rowan's hands tightened on the binoculars in excitement. One animal came up with a sea urchin in one paw and a flat rock in the other. It rolled onto its back and began hammering the sea urchin against the rock, then slurped out the innards as though eating ice cream from a cone.

Rowan pulled out her camera, focused the zoom lens and started clicking.

This was not river otter behaviour!

"Go slowly," she told herself. "Document carefully, or people aren't going to believe you."

If she could prove this kelp bed was the home of an endangered species, maybe she could prevent the island from being sold.

Rowan's field notes

Wednesday 3rd July

> *Five otters in the kelp bed.*
>
> *Lots of activity. Otters swimming up to the surface of the water and back down under the shiny brown kelp. They seem to be feeding. Their mouths are constantly in motion chewing fish and clams. They use their hands like we do, but they're pretty messy eaters.*
>
> *As I watched, one otter came up with a sea urchin and a flat rock. He (I don't know how to tell) placed the rock on his chest then started hammering the sea urchin on it to crack open the shell. Then he shlurped out the inside (poor sea urchin) and obviously loved it. Next it washed. The otter rolled over and over in the water, rubbed its face and cleaned its pelt, then shook its head and all the water drops fanned out from its whiskers. I guess that's what I saw the first time I noticed them.*
>
> *The otters roll around in the kelp until they are wrapped in it like seat belts. Then they lie on their backs and groom each*

other. They make me laugh.

They seem to spend a lot of time grooming their fur. They can't be looking for fleas like monkeys do, but it sure looks like it.

Another sea otter in the middle of the kelp is not quite as active as the main group. It looks as if there is something wrong. It's a funny shape.

It's a mother with a baby lying on her chest!

They are both sleeping in the sunshine.

While I watched she gently detached the baby, rolled it rapidly in kelp, then dived down into the water.

I didn't know what was happening because the baby started shrieking. I thought something must be wrong, but the other otters didn't seem disturbed. A few minutes later the mother popped up with some fish. She ate, then washed, then unrolled the baby and placed it on her chest again. It instantly stopped screaming and nuzzled with its head. I guess it was nursing.

This has been a most astonishing day...

Chapter Seven

"Hey Rowan! Surprise!"

The shout that came echoing through the trees wasn't Grant's voice. It sounded like Bevan. He must have sailed over instead. She rushed headlong down the path to meet him.

"Bevan, Bevan, I've something wonderful to show you."

"Hey watch it kid, we'll drop the surprise." Bevan held out a restraining arm as she skidded to a halt on the steep trail.

"Stop calling me kid," said Rowan in exasperation. "And what's all that stuff?" She looked at the boxes that Bevan was carrying. Behind him staggered Hoy, smiling over the top of a similar box. They seemed heavy.

Before either youth could answer there was a stealthy rustling in the bushes beside them. Rowan looked around.

"Take no notice," whispered Hoy. "It's the CIA."

Right on cue the twins emerged, creeping through the trees to Rowan's right. Despite the warmth of the afternoon they wore trench coats with the collars turned up and each carried a briefcase. They ignored everyone completely and headed off on their own.

"Why the secret service?" whispered Rowan.

"They are spies setting up a secret transmitting station. Between them, Hoy's father and the brats have come up with a really great idea."

Rowan looked doubtful. "You mean Morse code and stuff?" Bevan laughed and thankfully dumped the box in the middle of the clearing. "No, much easier. A plain and simple two-way radio. I should have thought of it myself. It should be more successful than the cell phone."

The twins reappeared, and stealthily climbed the large maple tree, pulling out and dropping the previous day's wire behind them.

"Do they know what they're doing?" asked Rowan doubtfully.

Bevan ruffled her hair. "They're unstringing the antenna they put up yesterday. They don't need it. This radio will be just the thing for you. The battery's powerful enough to transmit to our place."

The silence was rudely shattered by a yell from above.

Everyone's eyes shot upwards.

Martin was swinging by one hand trying to catch the wire with the other. "Over here, you dingbat," he screamed to Pat, forgetting about their vow of secrecy and silence.

The group below held their breath while Pat tossed the wire. Martin, swinging wildly, caught it and managed to hook his legs back on the branch in a less precarious position.

Peace resumed.

"It looks complicated," said Rowan as she doubtfully

eyed the radio. "Will I be able to work it when you've left?"

"Dead easy," Bevan reassured her. "All you have to remember is to flick the switch over before you talk and then back again when the other person talks."

"We'll demonstrate for you," Hoy assured her. "We already have a transmitter and receiver set up at the house. When this end is fixed, you'll be in radio communication with Anne and Grant."

"It sounds fun," grinned Rowan.

Hoy unpacked the boxes and efficiently connected up the transmitter and battery.

"Where did you get all the equipment from?" asked Rowan. "Isn't it expensive?"

Hoy looked up with a grin. "Not when you have a dad who owns one of the biggest radio parts factories in Hong Kong," he said.

Rowan gasped, "How could you get this over from Hong Kong? You only knew I was coming here yesterday!"

"No, no," Hoy reassured her, "this didn't come from Hong Kong. It's from our warehouse in Vancouver. My father is over here at the moment. I phoned him last night and explained what we needed. He flew out with it this morning. He was coming anyway as he had an appointment with some real estate people."

"Real estate people were out surveying this island today. They came over in a powerboat and were cruising around checking everything out."

Bevan nodded. "Yes, Mr. Symchuk wants to sell as soon as possible. I think he really needs the money."

"I hope he doesn't sell to someone who wants to chop down all the trees and build a hotel or something," grumbled Rowan. "There is so much wildlife here. Besides... this place is special. I tried to tell you but we got distracted with the radio... I've seen sea otters."

"You'll see otters maybe." Bevan shook his head. "But not sea otters. They live much farther north."

"That's what I thought," said Rowan slowly. "But do ordinary otters lie on their backs and break open sea urchins with small rocks?"

There was a moment's silence as Bevan and Hoy looked at each other and then at Rowan.

"You watched them doing that?" said Bevan, astonished.

Rowan nodded.

"Maybe they *are* sea otters," said Hoy. "I would love to see them."

Bevan straightened up. "Well, there is one way to find out. Let's get the radio fixed, then we'll see if they are still around."

The twins slid down the tree and stood before Hoy saluting smartly. "Antenna removed, sir," Pat reported. "Ready for the test transmission on your equipment."

Hoy nodded solemnly. "Good work men." He fiddled with some dials on the boxes and there were sounds of static. When he found the correct frequency he looked over at Rowan with a grin. "What code name are you going to use?"

"How about Otter Outlook?" suggested Rowan quickly before the twins could interrupt.

Hoy nodded and flicked a switch. "Base, this is Otter Outlook calling. Base, this is Rowan from Otter Outlook calling. Come in please. Over."

Hoy switched over and everyone strained to hear.

A voice came over the airwaves. Tiny and distant at first until Hoy adjusted the knobs, then clear and recognizable as Anne.

"Otter Outlook, this is base. Receiving you loud and clear. Well done Hoy. How is everything there Rowan? Over."

Rowan took the mike and flicked the switch. "Rowan here. Everything is wonderful and this radio makes it perfect. Like my code? It refers to the otters I saw today. I think they *are* sea otters. We're going to check them out. Over."

"Sounds unlikely, Rowan. Don't get your hopes up. Now, can you arrange to call us every evening at six? Then if you need anything we can sail across while it's still light. Over."

"I'd like to, but I haven't got a clock." Bevan nudged her and pointed to Martin lifting one out of the boxes. "Yes I have," she laughed. "Martin's just given me one. You think of everything. I'll call you at six. Over and out."

"Bye Rowan. Over and out from base." The radio fell silent.

"That was great," burbled Rowan as she turned around to the cousins. Then she saw the disapproving looks from Martin and Pat. "What's wrong?"

"Over and out," mimicked Martin. "Over and out. Whose idea was it for you to have a radio in the first place?"

"Yeah, don't we count?" asked Pat angrily. "What happened to our turn?"

Rowan looked crestfallen. "I'm sorry, I didn't think. I was just excited talking to Anne and trying to remember how to do it, and trying not to waste the battery. Tell you what. It's only around four now. You can call at six for the practice run. OK?"

The twins nodded.

"OK, but we do it on our own," said Pat.

"Yup. No help from anyone," challenged Martin.

The older group laughed and Rowan raised her hands in capitulation. "We promise."

"Right," said Bevan. "Let's go and see if we can find Rowan's sea otters."

It was idyllic up on the cliff. The sun had warmed the air and the rocks so that the light breeze from the sea felt pleasantly cool. Even the mosquitoes were too drowsy to bite. The sunlight danced and sparkled on the water and everything was almost too good to be true. Rowan was scared the otters would no longer be there, but to her relief they immediately spotted two playing and splashing in the kelp bed, and the others surfaced within a couple of minutes.

"That's impressive," said Hoy looking through the binoculars, and even the twins gazed in fascination.

The otters were totally oblivious to the watchers on the cliff. They fished, played and ate, emitting high-pitched squeals and whistles.

"Watch the mother... there she is... right on the edge of the kelp bed," whispered Rowan. "See how she wraps the young one up in its ribbons."

"Why does she do that?" asked Pat. "Is it cold?"

"No, it's so the baby won't float away and get lost while she dives to the bottom to feed," replied Rowan. "I read an article about it in *Nature Canada*. I never thought I'd get to see it though."

Bevan slapped her on the back. "Well Rowan, looks like you were right. So this island is home to a rare protected species. Now what?"

The island smiled and stretched like a cat in the sunlight, the Girl and her friends were listening. Around its edge the kelp beds swayed in an endless dance hiding and protecting the secret. Then a cloud obscured the sun and a shiver ran through the cedars. The change was about to begin.

Chapter Eight

With a roar, the peace was rudely shattered, as the sound of an approaching powerboat cut through the air.

Rowan sprang to her feet. "Oh no!" she cried. "The real estate people! If they come too near the kelp bed it will disturb the otters." She ran along the edge of the cliff waving her arms and yelling at the top of her voice.

It was no use. No one on the boat could hear above the noise of the engine. The powerboat screamed round the headland and through the edge of the kelp. There was a flurry of foam as the sea otters dove for safety—all except the young one tied to the kelp.

"No, no," yelled Rowan.

The group on the cliff watched helplessly as a small dark body was flung up by the propeller and then disappeared below the wake with only a tinge of red to show where it had been.

Rowan froze on the cliff edge. White faced and silent the twins were rooted to the spot, and even Bevan looked shaken to the core.

The boat below cruised around the cove unaware of the disaster in its wake. One of the people looked up, and seeing the group on the cliff top, gave a friendly wave as the boat sped off again.

Rowan gave a heart renching sob and Hoy placed his arm around her shoulder.

The sickening shock turned to anger.

"Murderers," yelled Martin angrily, shaking his fists. "Bloody, bloody murderers."

"We've got to do something. Those poor, poor, sea otters," sniffed Rowan, blowing her nose. "This island *must* be protected. No one should be able to kill them. Even by accident."

"We need a council of war," said Pat darkly.

"Yes, and someone to spy on the real estate people. Find out who they're trying to sell to," offered Martin.

"We really need someone who knows about the environmental protection laws," suggested Hoy.

Rowan looked tearfully at Hoy and Bevan. "Well, you two are the ones at law school," she said. "What can you find out?"

"We should check first on the status of sea otters, whether they *are* a protected species and how unusual it is to find them in this area," said Bevan thoughtfully. "I have a friend at the marine biology station in Victoria. I can do that tomorrow."

"OK, I'll phone my father," said Hoy. "I'll ask him to go to the real estate office and find out about this island and what kind of development it's zoned for. That way we'll know what we're up against."

Rowan blew her nose again and pulled herself together.

"I'll continue taking photos and making notes about the sea otters," she suggested. "We'll use them as proof to back up our claims."

"Right, and we'll lay traps and sabotage any one who tries to buy the island," said Martin eagerly.

"No way," said Bevan, Rowan and Hoy in chorus.

"We can't do anything unlawful," explained Bevan. "If we want to get this place considered a nature reserve or a protected area, we have to work within the law and impress people who count. If big money is involved we are going to have a tough job convincing investors that a bunch of kids have important information."

"I know," said Pat eagerly. "We need the newspapers on our side. Darcy has a friend at the *Island Times*."

"That's only a tiny newspaper," said Martin scornfully. What we want is the *Vancouver Sun* or the *Globe and Mail*. And how about the TV? I bet CBC would do a story." He picked up a twig and stuck it under Rowan's nose like a microphone. "Now tell me, Ms. Feldman, just how did you come to notice these rare animals?"

Rowan gave a shaky smile and put her arms around the twin's shoulders as they walked back to the cabin. "Thanks for helping guys," she said. "Listen. It's nearly six, and you wanted to use the radio. Why don't you ask your parents if you can come over tomorrow. That way you can keep an eye on the real estate people while I make the notes on the otters."

Both boys gave a yell of delight, thumped Rowan affectionately on the shoulders and raced ahead to the radio.

"Think you can handle them?" asked Bevan with a grin.

Rowan nodded. "It might be good to have someone else around while all this is happening. That way we know what's going on."

"We'll get Darcy involved too, she's only working part time," nodded Bevan. "With everyone helping we should be able to muster quite an impressive argument."

"If we *are* up against the development business we'll need it," said Hoy. "And a lot of luck."

That evening, after everyone had left, Rowan wandered unhappily down to the beach. The day that had started out so wonderfully had ended in disaster. She gazed sadly across the cove towards the setting sun. It was such a beautiful place. Ugly things shouldn't happen here. The sun's evening rays formed a golden path over the water, almost to her feet. But over the gentle sounds of the ocean she could hear the keening cries of the mother otter searching for her young.

Rowan walked to the edge of the waves and looked across at the kelp bed, but couldn't see anything against the setting sun.

The island sighed softly and sadly, and the waves gathered the baby sea sea otter into their embrace. Then, gently tossing the tiny battered body in a flurry of spume, the island laid the baby at the Girl's feet.

"Oh, I tried to stop them," Rowan cried out in despair, the tears rolling unchecked down her cheeks. She stepped into the tideways, ignoring the wet and the cold, and lifted the small sodden body to her heart.

Rowan searched for some broad ribbons of kelp and

tenderly wrapped the baby, covering the ugly gashes along its side, but leaving its tiny face free.

She carried it above the tideline.

Laying the limp little parcel on a log, Rowan scouted for a drift of sand sheltered by large pieces of driftwood, but within the sight and sound of the sea. Using a flat piece of driftwood, she dug a deep grave and carefully buried the baby sea otter. She finally patted and smoothed the small mound and covered the top with a design of shells and white pebbles and the sea thrift flowers growing nearby. Then she leaned back on her heels and made a solemn promise.

"Never again, little sea otter," she whispered. "I'll do my best to see that this never happens again." She softly sang the snatches of a song from deep in her childhood memory.

> Oh hush thee my child
> On the waves born along
> The twilight is darkening
> Oh hear the wind's song.
> Over the tideways, over the sea,
> Wrapped safe you will slumber,
> Safe home to me.

The breeze sighed and the waves wept and the drifts of evening mist took the cobwebs of music and spun them into the nightly shroud around the island. The endless cycle was repeating and a slaughter had happened again. But this time there was hope and a witness. The Girl was here, her tears were mingling with the tears of the island. Maybe this time the slaughter could be stopped.

Chapter Nine

Grant and Anne Jenner were sitting in Mr. Symchuk's kitchen deep in a difficult conversation.

"Yes, we know you need to sell the island, Mr. Symchuk," said Grant patiently. "But we were wondering if you had considered selling the island to a foundation as a wildlife preserve or nature reserve, rather than to a developer."

"Developers are the only ones who have money these days," snorted Mr. Symchuk. "All those nature reserve people want you to *give* them the land. What good would that do me?"

"When did you last go and see the island?" asked Anne.

There was a pause while Mr. Symchuk thought. "Well now, I guess it was when you were painting over there, Anne."

"But that was nineteen years ago," said Anne in dismay. "No wonder you've forgotten how beautiful it is. Why don't we take you out there? Then you can see the sea otters for yourself."

"Look young woman," Mr. Symchuk wheezed. "I'm an old man, and I need money. The island is the only thing I have left to sell. Seeing it again isn't going to make one jot of difference."

"Yes, but will you come with us?" Anne persisted. "Wouldn't you like to see it again?"

There was a pause as Mr. Symchuk thought it over. "Alright. I *would* like to see the place again. I could come on Sunday."

Anne and Grant nodded their agreement

"But it won't make any difference you know," he added sadly "It has to go."

"OK, we'll meet you on the dock on Sunday, just before noon. We will put a lunch together for everyone, so all you have to do is turn up," said Anne.

Anne and Grant strolled thoughtfully back to their house.

"Why?" said Anne forcefully. "Why does Mr. Symchuk suddenly need money so desperately? I always thought he was quite well off."

Grant hugged her. "Now now, you are not to ask him," he warned. "It's none of our business."

"I know, but he always loved the island. He once told me he was going to keep it for his grandchildren. I can't imagine what has changed his mind."

"We may never know," said Grant, "but he has a perfect right to sell his own property. All we can can hope for is that there is a buyer out there who is sensitive enough to want to protect the environment."

Anne nodded in agreement. "The kids seem to think they can save the island. I don't know whether they've thought about it from Mr. Symchuk's point of view."

"Well, they'll meet him on Sunday," said Grant with a grin. "Should be an interesting day."

Darcy was working an evening shift at her part-time job in the Tofino coffee shop, but there were very few customers. She checked they were all served, than took her break with her friend Vikki who worked for the community newspaper *Island Times*. Darcy sat down at Vikki's table and tried to coax her to do a story on the sea otters.

"Come on, Vikki," she argued. You give space to community events, weddings, marina developments, even who's on a Caribbean cruise—why not do a local interest animal story?"

"Look, Darcy," said Vikki bluntly, "whoever heard of sea otters around there? I think your cousin is mixed up. Did you identify them?"

"No," admitted Darcy, "but Bevan did. And my parents are going out to see them tomorrow."

"My editor would kill me if I spent time and space on a major story that proved to be incorrect," continued Vikki. "Tell you what, though. Give me a call tomorrow night after your parents have made a positive identification. If they really are sea otters I'll do a full two-page spread next week complete with photos, OK?"

"OK," agreed Darcy."But don't blame me if you miss the scoop of a lifetime."

No one could get through to the Jenner's house that evening; both the internet and telephone lines were constantly buzzing.

Bevan sat at the computer. As he determinedly worked his way through cyberspace, the printer slowly engulfed him with piles of paper.

"Do you want the good news or the bad?" he asked eventually.

Hoy looked up from his phone conversation.

"Sea otters *are* protected, but under marine protection laws. Looks to me like it's nothing to do with land."

"Did you hear that Dad?" Hoy spoke into the phone again. "Now where is that going to leave us?"

"Thank goodness everyone's finally off the phone," grumbled Pat. How come we're always the last to use it?"

"Yeah, first it was the parents, then Bevan and Hoy talking to the marine biological station, then Hoy calling his dad, then Bevan again, then Hoy," agreed Martin. "And we've a really important call to make before it gets too late. Come on everyone, now it's our turn.... Please!"

"In secret," added Pat pointedly.

Bevan and Hoy grinned and left the room.

Back on Otter Island, Rowan tossed and turned restlessly. Finally she switched on her flashlight and took out her journal.

Friday, 5th July

> *Every time I close my eyes, I see the baby otter. It's the most horrible thing I have ever witnessed.*
>
> *I realized after I'd buried the body, that I should have taken a photo of it. Then we would have had a record, proof.*
>
> *I couldn't. It made me feel sick.*
>
> *Actually it didn't occur to me at the time. I was too upset, but Dad would have photographed it. He would have pushed his feelings aside and done his job. Guess I've got a lot to learn.*
>
> *Anne says Mr. Symchuk is coming to visit the island on Sunday. Maybe seeing the otters will change his mind.*
>
> *I'll show him my notes. If he realizes how important this place is, surely he'll do something.*
>
> *I should write some proper field notes, but I'm too upset. I'll write everything down tomorrow when I can think straight.*

Rowan finally settled down in her sleeping bag. Around her cabin, the island animals went about their nightly business. A deer and two fawns stepped daintily through the moonlit clearing, pausing only to sniff at the food splashes around the coleman stove, before melting back into the forest shadows. A mink rustled in the under-growth as it stalked a small vole, and a couple of bats swooped and dipped after insects. Rowan missed it all. But while she slept, and the animals worked, the wheels everyone had set in motion that evening, slowly and surely began to turn.

Silently the owl flew through the glade and perched watchfully on the cedar tree. It had done its job. Its mournful cry had called the name of the baby otter and death had followed. It mattered not that the Girl was unaware, she was playing her part well. The island waited patiently, encouragingly. The owl spread its wings and melted into the mist.

Chapter Ten

Katrina Vasey's powerboat puttered into the Jenner's landing.

Bevan poked his head out of *Nootka's* cockpit and looked across questioningly. "Hello... are you looking for someone?"

"Yes, the Jenners," Katrina shouted above the sound of the motor. "Could I dock and explain?"

"Sure." Bevan jumped out of *Nootka* and waited for Katrina to throw a rope.

She swung gently alongside the dock and turned off the engine. Tossing the stern rope to Bevan she leapt lightly down and secured the prow rope herself.

"Hi, I'm Katrina Vasey, a wildlife biologist from Vancouver Aquarium. Are you one of the Jenner family?" Katrina stuck out her hand.

"Yes, I'm Bevan Jenner. How did you get here so soon? I only e-mailed the aquarium last night."

"I was in the Tofino area and when I phoned in for messages this morning they read me yours." Katrina ran her finger through her hair excitedly. "I specialize in sea mammals. I was working here because several reports of sea otters came from this area. I asked around in Tofino and someone who'd been in the coffee shop remembered overhearing the waitress talking to Vikki from *Island Times*."

Bevan grinned. "That was my sister Darcy. It's a small town."

"Yes, that's what Vikki said! She gave me your phone number, but when I heard about your e-mail, I decided to come directly to meet you. So tell me what you think you've seen."

As they walked over to the house Bevan recounted the story. "We'll phone Rowan, then go over to the island and you can see for yourself," he finished.

An excited Rowan met them on the beach. "This is wonderful," she burbled. "Mr. Symchuck is coming over tomorrow and it would be great to have a positive identification by then." She led the way up to the lookout area and gestured to everyone to be quiet.

To her delight, the otters were waiting, wrapped in a raft of kelp, snoozing on their backs, paws in the air.

Katrina started shooting film, shot after shot.

"Wonderful," breathed Katrina. She looked up from her camera with sparkling eyes. "This is exactly what I was hoping for."

"So, what do we do now?" Rowan asked.

"I need to make some observations and do a head count," Katrina smiled across at Rowan. "I'd like to see your notes and photos too."

Rowan nodded happily. "Of course."

"And I need to dive to check out the health of the kelp bed. But that will have to wait as I'm on my own."

"We could help there," Bevan interjected.

Katrina looked across, interested.

"Both Rowan and I dive and I can handle a boat. We could come with you as support?"

"Have you got your power squadron certification?" Katrina asked Bevan.

Bevan nodded. "Mom and Dad insist we have all the mariner and diving courses. When you live out here it's almost a requirement."

Rowan found herself crossing her fingers behind her back and holding her breath.

Katrina considered a moment. "OK." She looked up at the sky. "The weather seems fairly settled. Rowan, would you like to be my dive partner, if Bevan will crew the boat?"

"Certainly," said Rowan in her most grown-up voice, but inside her heart was racing and she felt ready to burst with excitement.

It took time to cross the channel to the Jenners' to collect and check the equipment, but by afternoon they had everything together. They swiftly loaded Rowan's gear into the boat and swung aboard.

"All set?" Katrina asked.

"You bet."

Katrina set the engine in gear. They backed off smoothly from the dock and set off around Otter Island.

The channel was smooth and still, but the moment they rounded the corner of the island the swell became noticeable and the wind brisker.

"Want to take over?" Katrina asked Bevan.

She watched approvingly as Bevan competently brought the boat around the far side of the island.

Rowan's hair flapped in her face and she pulled an elastic out of her jeans pocket and tied it back.

"Heave to about fifty metres off the kelp bed," called Katrina over the noise of the motor. "I don't want to disturb the sea otters."

Bevan anchored and dropped the flagged buoy over the side to show there was a dive in progress while Rowan and Katrina swiftly suited up.

Rowan spat in her goggles and rinsed them out. "Brrr, the water's freezing," she said. "The last time I dived was in California."

"We'll go in on the far side of the boat then swim under toward the kelp bed and cliff," instructed Katrina. "I'll go first, but we must always stay in visual distance of each other. We will be staying at the base of the kelp. It's easy to get tangled in it so we have to be very slow and careful. If you do get caught, just disentangle calmly."

Rowan nodded. She pulled up the hood of her wet suit, slipped on the facemask and gave the thumbs up sign to Katrina.

They both slid over the side.

The cold water numbed Rowan's lips, clasped firmly around the mouthpiece of her breathing apparatus, and gave her body a brisk shock despite the wetsuit. She tensed, but gradually relaxed as the thin layer of water leaking into the wetsuit begin to warm against her skin. She consciously slowed her breathing as she sank beneath the waves and listened to the comforting sounds from the regulator and the stream of silvery bubbles.

Katrina waited until she was at the same level then pointed.

Rowan nodded and they both kicked down and forward.

Rowan swallowed hard to clear the pressure in her ears from the relentless pressure of the water. She always had to steel herself to get used to the pressure. Every dive her imagination ran riot thinking of the horror stories of early divers being squashed as flat as pancakes.

Suddenly the magic of the moment took over as it always did, and with a flick of her fins she was gliding over the ocean floor.

The sunlight filtered through the emerald sea highlighting the millions of minute organisms floating in clouds around them, and beneath her, the dancing red feather fronds of thousands of barnacles, their volcano-shaped shells clamped to the rocky bottom while their fronds gracefully pulled plankton from the water.

A few more kicks and there in front of them, hanging like a great yellow-brown curtain, was the kelp forest, each strand firmly anchored by a holdfast root to a large stone on the ocean floor. The strands stretched up to the light where they were suspended by a gas-filled bulb floating on the surface of the ocean. Three or four long broad ribbony blades spread like branches from the top of each stem. They swayed and danced enticingly.

Katrina and Rowan gently parted some thick strands on the edge of the kelp patch and slipped inside.

It was another world. Here the light was more subdued, with a strong play of shadows as the dancing kelp alternately cut out and let in the sun. Rowan was filled with wonder. It *was* a forest, with slim trunks and broad branches undulating gently in the current instead of swaying in a breeze.

No wonder the otters liked to live here, for the forest contained a living pantry. Kelp crabs and snails hung from its fronds and hundreds of fish swam within its shelter. The ocean floor around its roots provided delicious foraging. There were sea anemones and abalone, clams, oysters, tube worms and mussels, all vying for space, and above it all swayed the kelp in a graceful dance accompanied by darting fish and floating plankton.

Katrina pointed out the purple spiny sea urchins feeding on the kelp. Rowan pointed out a Dungeness crab groping its way across a stone and a giant orange sunstar with all sixteen legs splayed out.

Suddenly Katrina pointed upwards and Rowan turned.

A otter streamed down towards them. It didn't seem bothered by their intrusion, only intent on getting food. It picked up a flat rock from the bottom and tucked it in the loose skin under its arm, chose a suitable urchin and with a quick turn shot up to the surface again in a flurry of bubbles.

Katrina and Rowan happily gave each other the high five, then carried on their work, noting the species and checking out how well the kelp was established. Eventually they gently moved back out of the forest, helping disentangle each other as they went.

"Fantastic," said Rowan as Bevan helped relieve her of the breathing equipment. "Absolutely, incredibly, fantastic."

Katrina laughed. "Going to sign up as a marine biologist?" she teased.

Rowan looked at her seriously. "I might..." she said. "I just might...."

Katrina looked thoughtful as the two of them slipped out of their wet suits and into dry clothes, jostling for space in the boat's tiny cabin.

"Rowan, how long are you staying on Otter Island?"

"I've permission to be here three weeks in all..." Rowan pulled a warm sweater over her head and chuckled. "This was supposed to be a peaceful retreat, but it's been totally chaotic with all the excitement about the sea otters."

"Any chance you could be here all summer?" asked Katrina.

"I... I don't know... I don't know If I'd want to be on my own that long. Why?"

Katrina climbed out on deck and Rowan followed. They sat on the gunwales and lifted their faces to the sun.

"I was thinking," continued Katrina. "I have to go back to the office soon, but it would be really good to have someone here keeping an eye on things. An official volunteer who checks the otters everyday and notifies the aquarium if there are problems."

Bevan looked at Rowan. "That sounds like an extension of your project."

"Yes," agreed Rowan. "But...."

"What's the matter kid?"

"Quit calling me kid," Rowan blazed. "I'm not a kid, you should know that by now."

Katrina slipped to the back of the boat and busied herself checking the outboard.

Bevan looked startled. "Sorry... I didn't mean you were," He paused. "You're right. I won't do it again....Anyway, what *is* the matter?"

Rowan shook her head. "I don't really know. Guess I'm wondering what I should do. I don't really want to be on my own on the island all summer." She looked up at Bevan. "But helping Katrina as a volunteer is a great idea. Guess we'd have to clear it with Mr. Symchuck though."

Splashing from the kelp bed attracted their attention. They both watched as a couple of sea otters playfully rolled over and over each other.

"Bevan," asked Rowan shyly, "if Mr. Symchuck agrees, do you think you and Darcy and the rest of the family would be interested? All of us could volunteer and take it in turns?"

Bevan slipped his arm around her shoulders and gave her a friendly squeeze. "So you're not running away from us any more, eh?"

Rowan agreed happily. "No... You've all been so helpful. Guess. I'm ready to be part of your family after all."

Rowan's Field Notes

Sunday July 7th

Today I acted as Katrina Vasey's diving partner, and Bevan crewed the boat. Bevan noted the surface activities of the otters from the deck, while Katrina and I dived.

We were able to ascertain there are actually seven sea otters living together as a raft and Katrina thinks it's a group of females. All look healthy but unfortunately the pup that died seem to be the only offspring this year. However, it's impossible to tell if any of the other females are pregnant and one may have a late pup. This means there must be a group of males not far away. Katrina is going to search for them too.

Katrina and I spent an hour exploring the kelp and observing the sea otters.

We officially listed all the types of sea life we observed in and around the kelp forest and did a sea urchin count. I helped Katrina measure the forest's length and breadth. She feels it can support the otters that are there and that it should grow as the group grows.

Sea otters and sea urchins are intertwined. The otters eat the sea urchins, sea urchins eat the kelp. As long as the otters are keeping the urchin population under control, the kelp forest will expand.

Katrina says we lost thousands of kelp forests around our coast when the sea otters were hunted and wiped out. Because the sea urchins had no predator, they just ate the kelp unchecked. Once the kelp forests were gone, the safe habitat for many sea creatures was gone.

Until I dived with Katrina I had never thought of the kelp as a forest. It's changed my whole perception and view of the ocean.

There is an amazing difference between the amount of sea life outside the kelp forest and the teeming, jostling life within its protective shelter. I hadn't realized we need to preserve our ocean forests to keep the ocean healthy just as we need to preserve our trees to keep the earth healthy.

Katrina was teasing me about being a wildlife biologist. It isn't a joke. The otters are so fascinating. I just might become one.

Rowan closed her field notes and sat gazing thoughtfully over the glade. The evening shadows were closing in, but there was still an air of frantic activity as a bat and a couple of swallows swooped and dove, vying with each other for the evening insect hunt.

Not even a week, that's all it had been, but this tiny island had already changed her life. Rowan stood up and stretched then stepped outside the cabin.

She stepped lightly across the glade and laid her hand

on the bark of the giant cedar. The rough grain tickled her palm and the sharp fresh evergreen smell tantalized her nostrils. She imagined she could feel the coursing of the sap as it had for decades.

The island sent a shower of shooting stars across the velvet sky.

Chapter Eleven

There had been a shower overnight. Rowan poked her nose out of the cabin Sunday morning, to find the clearing sparkling and shining with tiny droplets that still clung to the grass blades and leaves, hanging the spider's webs with crystal beads. Even the air had that washed and scrubbed smell, a freshness of damp earth, spruce needles, and the sharp salty tang of wet seaweed. The sky was still misty, but hinted at a promise of the deep blue that would develop during the day.

Rowan's anxiety to impress Mr. Symchuk made her determined that everything should be impeccable. She finished all her house chores before breakfast. She swept, dusted, made the bed, freshened the flowers, and made sure not one item of rubbish could be seen; she even tidied loose twigs that had fallen from the trees, around the glade. As far as Rowan was concerned, Mr. Symchuk's island had to be a vision of paradise.

"Perfect," Rowan thought looking around with satisfaction. "Everything's ready."

Grabbing a cookie, Rowan raced with her camera and notebook up to the headland. As she reached her outlook point, the sun broke through the mist, burning it off in long gossamer streaks against a turquoise sky.

"By the time everyone's sailed over I'll have all the notes ready and I'll have finished the film," she decided. "Maybe Bevan or Darcy can get it developed for me."

Carefully and concisely she added her current observations.

The morning passed very quickly on her cliff top. Despite the loss of the young one from their group, most of the otters were very active, fishing, grooming and enjoying the fine weather. Today there were six of them playing among the kelp. Only one seemed to be listless.

"That must be the mother otter," observed Rowan. "Poor thing. I wonder if animals understand when accidents happen? I wonder how long she'll mourn?"

Right on time, as the sun hit the noon heights, she heard *Nootka*. The boat did a circuit of the the island. Rowan waved as they passed the headland. *Nootka* avoided the kelp beds, but paused near them. Rowan could see Bevan through her binoculars. He was pointing out the sea otters to a white-haired man on deck.

"So that's Mr. Symchuk," thought Rowan as she studied him carefully through the binoculars. His hair ruffled in the breeze and he smoothed it off his face with a gnarled hand. "Hmm, he looks like my grandfather." Rowan felt her spirits rise and she left the cliff and headed around to the inlet to meet them.

Pat and Martin rowed the dinghy and helped Mr. Symchuk and Darcy onto the beach.

Mr. Symchuk came forward, hand outstretched.

"So you're the young woman who's causing all the fuss," he grunted, but softened it by giving Rowan's hand a friendly pat.

"Yes sir. I'm Rowan. Did you see the sea otters?"

"Briefly. They dived as the boat came past then surfaced again and looked at us. They are curious little beggars. Bevan tells me you will take me up to your look-out after lunch?"

Rowan nodded and was about to launch into a passionate plea for the island when Mr. Symchuk fore-stalled her. "I'm glad I said I'd come and see the island, and watch the otters," he said. "I think they're wonderful."

Everyone looked at each other with astonished faces.

Mr. Symchuk looked piercingly at Rowan. "But it won't make any difference, you know. The island has to be sold."

There was a collective sigh of disappointment, and Rowan opened her mouth again, then stopped.

Something in Mr. Symchuk's gaze, a hint of pain in the faded blue depths of his eyes, made Rowan drop the subject and look away. Her mind was in turmoil. She instinctively liked Mr. Symchuk, but desperately wanted to stop the island from being sold. She felt her own eyes grow moist as a vision of the baby otter rose up before her.

Darcy slid up beside her and placed her arm around Rowan's waist and gave a friendly squeeze. "Well, you certainly found a project Rowan. More than you bargained for I guess. Mom suggested we should all have lunch first. Then we could walk out to the headland and discuss the otters."

Rowan nodded and gave a shaky smile, grateful for the

distraction. Besides, lunch would give her time to assess Mr. Symchuk and figure out the best way of reaching him.

Grant and Bevan had formed a circle of rocks on the beach and lit a small driftwood fire within them. The twins were already roasting wieners, and as Rowan, Darcy and Mr. Symchuk walked over, Anne handed them wire coat hangers to use as roasting forks for their own sausages. For a while everyone was busy, cooking, eating and relaxing under the summer skies.

Mr. Symchuk wiped his mouth and tossed his paper napkin into the glowing embers. "Haven't roasted wieners for years, Anne. Not since my kids were small. Thanks. That was a lot of fun." Then he looked around at the group. "Look, I'm not much for blabbing my troubles around. But I'm going to take you folks into my confidence." He looked sharply at everyone. "That means I'm going to trust you not to blab."

Everyone nodded solemnly, but Anne jumped in. "You don't have to explain, Mr. Symchuk. It's really none of our business."

Mr. Symchuk nodded. "No it's not, except that you people have enjoyed the island for years. And you've looked after it and kept it as natural as possible. I've been really impressed with the way you have respected the land. That's why I've always allowed you to come here. I was glad that someone took the same pleasure in it that I did in my younger days."

Mr. Symchuk blew his nose firmly and carried on. "I'm putting the island on the market. I don't want to sell it to developers, but that's who's got the money to buy it." He looked around. "You must admit it would make a lovely place for a hotel. It's got fresh water, a sheltered inlet for a boat and plane, wonderful views, and is in reach of the city. Should sell well." He shrugged. "It's really unfortunate that young Rowan here discovered it's a haven for the sea otters."

Mr. Symchuk stood up and stretched. "Figured I owe you an explanation. So you understand why I can't do anything about the otters." He fiddled in his pocket and brought out a couple of photos. "These are my grandchildren. I'd always intended to leave the island to them." He passed the photos around.

"Now Julie is doing fine. She nine. Coming along nicely." Mr. Symchuk pointed to the other picture. "But twelve-year-old Jaimie, he's a different kid—autistic they call it. Can't relate to people and needs a special kind of schooling. He's been going to a special school in Nanaimo, but now he's older and bigger, it's not working out."

"Jaimie gets angry and frustrated. He scares little Julie and because he's growing so big it's almost getting more than my daughter can handle. We've heard of a new place that might be able to help him. It's in the States and it's expensive—it's one-on-one treatment. The school district can't afford to do that. Neither can my daughter. I said I'd help, send them all down there for a year, maybe longer."

He sighed and spread out his hands in a helpless gesture. "What's the good of saving an island for a child that won't be able to appreciate it, unless he gets the right kind of help now? See, I've no choice. To help Jaimie I have to sell the island." He sighed again and held his hands up in despair.

The group around the campfire was wrapped in

thought. Then Darcy patted Mr. Symchuk's arm. "We understand," she said. "You're quite the grandfather."

Everyone had been so intent listening to Mr. Symchuk that no one had noticed an approaching whirring sound. Suddenly the clatter of a small helicopter sounded right overhead. Everyone looked up. The helicopter took a turn around the island, then came back. It hovered over the headland and started to descend.

"Goodness, who's that?" gasped Anne, and looked around at the family. Pat and Martin were looking very uncomfortable.

"We're sorry, Mr. Symchuk," stuttered Pat. "We didn't know about Jaimie."

"Boys, what have you done? Who is that?" thundered Grant.

"It's the ITV news team," explained Martin, very embarrassed. "We phoned them last night. They've come to do a 'Save the Sea Otter' story!"

Chapter Twelve

Everybody looked aghast, then fixed accusing eyes on the twins.

"Now you've really done it," said Bevan. "What are we going to tell them? Mr. Symchuk asked us not to blab."

"No use crying over spilt milk," said Anne briskly. "The ITV news team is here. We'll show them the otters, and leave it at that. Think you can handle it Rowan? They might not stay too long if they think only young people are involved."

Rowan nodded. "But what happens when they ask me why the island is being sold?"

Mr. Symchuk sighed heavily. "Just tell them I can't afford to keep it any longer. It's the truth anyway!"

"Pat and Martin, I don't want to hear or see you until we're rid of the ITV people," Grant said sternly.

The two boys nodded. Their shoulders drooped with dejection. "We're sorry," they whispered. "We were only trying to help the otters; we didn't want to hurt anyone."

Grant looked at the rest of the group "This has to be a

positive story that will enhance the right kind of interest in the island," he continued. "If people get up in arms about it, it will cause real trouble for Mr. Symchuk and affect the sale."

Rowan stood up. "Well, I guess I'd better go up and meet the ITV people on the headland, so they don't come down here."

"We'll come with you," offered Bevan and Darcy.

"Mr. Symchuk, come to the cabin," suggested Anne. "We'll wait there until we hear the helicopter take off again, then we can rejoin the others."

The group on the beach rapidly dispersed, leaving Pat and Martin looking at each other.

"What do we do?" asked Martin, moodily skimming a stone on the waves and watching it bounce.

"What we normally do, idiot," said Pat thumping him on the back. "Spy on everyone to see what's going on." The two boys grinned at each other, melted silently into the forest, and up one of their hidden trails.

"Hello there, have you come to check out the sea otters?" asked Rowan cheerfully.

"Yes, I'm Maxine Summers of ITV. Do you mind if we ask you a few questions?"

The cameraman stalked silently around. He leaned over the cliff to zoom in for otter shots, then moved around the headland and intercut shots of Rowan during her on-camera interview with the news anchorwoman.

Rowan handled the ITV people with aplomb, pointing

out the kelp bed and its occupants and vividly describing how she first saw the otters and realized what they were.

Maxine turned to Bevan. "So you've been researching the status of the sea otters and have verified they are an endangered species?" Bevan nodded and explained his strategy.

"Have we got everything here?" Maxine looked questioningly at the cameraman who nodded. "Let's get some shots down on the beach to wrap up."

Sighing, Rowan showed the news team the path.

"We've got to do something," she hissed as she passed Darcy. "They'll see the grave and then we're into another set of explanations."

Darcy nodded and quickly vanished.

The team walked onto the beach to find Darcy sitting on a log with a towel draped behind her. Rowan gave the thumbs up sign and turned her attention to the cameras again.

"We realize this island has to be sold, but we are hoping that there is someone out there who could buy it and protect the otters," Rowan finished.

As though waiting for its cue, a breeze sprang up and whipped and flapped at the towel behind Darcy.

There was the pathetic little grave in full view, sea shells gleaming and the sadly faded sea thrift reflecting the care and sorrow that had gone into its making.

The cameraman immediately focused on it. Maxine looked questioningly at Rowan, who flushed.

"I don't really want to discuss it," she said uncomfortably and shuffled her feet.

"So it's to do with the otters?" said Maxine shrewdly.

"Did one of them die?"

Rowan's face flamed and her eyes watered. She felt pressured into saying something. Haltingly she gave the simple facts. "But it was an accident," she emphasized. "We don't want people to get mad at Mr. Symchuk, who needs to sell the island."

"Fantastic," said the cameraman. "There won't be a dry eye in the house by the time we've got this lot cut and edited. This should help your cause, not hinder it..." and he started to dismantle his camera and battery.

Thankful that the interview was over Rowan said a subdued goodbye to Maxine and the cameraman, and helped them find the trail back up the headland and the helicopter.

Suddenly the afternoon's peace was shattered yet again, this time by the roar of a powerboat.

The twins erupted onto the path, panting and sweating in their hurry. "Hey everyone," they yelled at the top of their lungs. "The real estate boat is back again. We've been looking through the binoculars. There's several people on board and Hoy is one of them!"

Chapter Thirteen

Rowan held her breath as the power boat approached the headland, but this time it slowed down and gave the kelp bed a wide berth.

"Thank goodness," breathed Rowan. "Hoy must have told them about the otters." She looked at the twins. "You two better run to the cabin and warn everyone there," she suggested. "The boat is obviously going to land people on the beach."

The twins raced back the way they had come and vanished over the brow of the headland. The cameraman looked at the anchorwoman who gave him a brief nod. He reshouldered his camera.

"Hey, I thought you folks were leaving!" said Rowan in dismay.

"Not when we smell another part to the story," said the anchor woman with a charming smile. "We'd like to see who else is here."

Rowan and Darcy looked helplessly at each other.

Bevan squared his shoulders and stepped forward.

"We've given you the story," he said politely but firmly. "This is private property. We are asking you to leave. Now, please."

Maxine raised her eyebrows. "Oh! Are you the owner? Can you ask us to leave? Or are you here as a guest, just as we are?"

Bevan looked thoughtfully at her. "No, I'm here at the invitation of the owner. Are you?"

Maxine shrugged. There was a feeling of tension in the air.

Bevan smiled. "Come on," he said. "You and I both know you have to leave private property upon request. There is nothing else to tell you at the moment. How about we contact you if there are new developments?"

The group watched silently as the news team climbed into the helicopter, and it took off in a flurry of wind and noise.

Darcy and Rowan turned admiringly to Bevan.

"Wow, you were fantastic. Like a real lawyer," said Darcy.

"I wish I could have handled things as well as you did," said Rowan. "I tried not to talk too much, but she was so nosy."

"You did fine," Bevan said. "Handling the press isn't easy."

"Guess we'd better go and see what else needs handling," said Rowan. "My quiet retreat is turning into a circus."

The powerboat rode at anchor in the bay, and Hoy and an older Chinese man were clambering over the rubber rim of the small Zodiac that had ferried them to the beach.

With rolled up jeans and sandals slung around their shoulders, they looked very relaxed. Rowan waved.

"Rowan, come and meet my father, Mr. Chan," called Hoy, and pointed to the man beside him, who, despite his casual situation, bowed formally to her.

"*Nai ho ma*," said Rowan repeating the bow.

Mr. Chan beamed, stepped forward and pumped her hands, then gazed in amazement at a point behind her.

Rowan heard chanting and turned around.

Two pairs of legs were marching along the beach, topped by large pieces of cardboard saying: OTTERS OTTER BE LEFT ALONE

"Otters ought to be left alone, otters ought to be left alone," chanted the twins in unison as they halted in front of the Zodiac.

With a great clatter the ITV helicopter swooped over head. The cameraman hung out of the window shooting the scene on the beach before the helicopter swung off to disappear behind the trees.

Bevan cursed under his breath.

"Pat... Martin... quit it!" Grant's roar cut through the noise.

The twins stopped and lowered the cardboard, looking hurt.

The rest of the family, followed by a panting Mr. Symchuk, arrived on the beach with a rush.

Grant pulled the twins back and relieved them of the placards. They stood to one side looking sulky.

"We were only trying to help," said Pat in an injured voice.

Grant glared. "Let's hope you've not done irretrievable damage."

Politeness took over again and Rowan and Hoy continued the introductions, but before Hoy could explain his father's presence on the island they were joined by a third person.

"Hi folks. Busy place for a small island." Despite having rolled up his trousers to splash through the shallows, the man, obviously a realtor, managed to retain his city polish. "I'm Mike Newman, from People's Realty. Nice surprise to see you here, Mr. Symchuk. Guess you already met my client Mr. Chan."

The two men nodded to each other.

"Wonderful property." Mike Newman swept his arm around expansively to encompass the whole Island. "I was just telling Mr. Chan what a fabulous recreational place this cove would make. You could situate a small hotel up on the hill—just clear all those trees to get the view. The inlet on the other side could house a marina, no problem. This place has everything."

Everyone looked silently at the ground.

Rowan felt a lump in her throat. She'd thought Hoy was her friend. Encouraging his father to consider the island for a hotel development wasn't going to help. She shuffled her feet and heard a voice, barely recognizable as her own, say, "If you made a resort here, what would happen to the sea otters?"

"Cute little beggars aren't they?" Newman jumped in enthusiastically. "Guests would really enjoy watching them. We've got some in the bay near our place. We go and watch them play in the evening. They've made a slide on the bank just like kids."

He turned to Mr. Chan. "Could be a real attraction, sir."

"No, you don't understand. These aren't river otters. These are sea otters. They're rare, a protected species. We think this is the first time they have colonized in this area in this century. If this island is developed it might drive them away," said Rowan passionately.

"Aw, come on kid," said Newman, patting her arm in a friendly fashion. "They'd just go somewhere else. No one's going to hurt them."

Rowan moved away as though she had been stung.

"Oh yeah," said Martin derisively, "then how come you already killed one?"

Anne and Grant both stepped forward as the realtor looked startled.

"That's enough, Martin," said Grant firmly. "It was an accident." Anne took Martin to one side and whispered in his ear.

"But it's true," burst out Pat in defense of his twin. He pointed to the realtor. "You murdered a baby otter two days ago. Sure it was an accident. But your boat's propeller hit one. If this island's developed there'll be more accidents like that and the otters will disappear again. They need to be protected."

The real estate man took a gold-plated cigarette case out of his pocket and handed it around. Everyone shook their heads, but he removed one, lit it and slowly and deliberately drew on it.

"I'd be real careful about asking for protection for any wildlife if I were you," he said, looking across at Mr. Symchuk. "Do that and you'll never sell."

"Then what will happen to Jaimie," thought Rowan as Mr. Symchuk half raised his hands in despair and walked alone to a nearby log and sat gazing into the distance.

Mr. Chan stood impassively. Only his dark eyes moved as he intently watched everyone's reactions.

"Oh no!" Bevan groaned and pointed to the bay. A small sailing dinghy was tacking in. "Tourists. That's just what we need." He looked across at Mr. Symchuk. "Want me to head them off, sir?"

Mr. Symchuk nodded, and Bevan strode purposefully to the water's edge. "Sorry folks, you can't land. This is private property," he called. A tousled head looked around the sail.

"Don't be an idiot, Bevan. It's me, Vikki, Darcy's friend from *Island Times*."

Vikki turned and pointed to a slim figure steering in the back of the boat. "And you've already met Katrina Vasey, the wildlife biologist. We've come out to meet Mr. Symchuk."

Bevan threw up his hands in despair and stomped up the beach. "How many more people are involved in this?" he demanded. "We could be repelling boarders all day. Who else in this crazy family has told someone who wants to make us front-page news."

Anne started to laugh. It started as a small chuckle and grew. Grant joined in and then, despite themselves, everyone on the beach found themselves laughing.

"I'm sorry," stuttered Anne, wiping her streaming eyes. "But this is such a ridiculous situation." She walked over to Mr. Symchuk and sat beside him, her hand on his knee.

"Mr. Symchuk, can we have your permission to take everyone here into our confidence? Otherwise this whole silly situation is going to get out of hand."

Mr. Symchuk gave a barely perceptible nod. "If you think it's wise," he said quietly.

"OK," said Anne firmly. "It's time to talk. There are no villains in this piece, just people working on different sides of the same problem without seeing the whole. Now let's see what we can figure out together."

Chapter Fourteen

Darcy, Bevan, and Rowan heaved driftwood logs around the remaining embers of the fire so everyone could sit down in an extended circle. The laughter had lessened the tensions, and the circle made the oddly-assorted group seem more of a team. Only the realtor seemed the odd person out. He shuffled uncomfortably, aware that he was not very popular with at least two-thirds of the group.

"OK, who's going to start?" he asked, flashing a big grin to cover his discomfort.

Anne looked at Rowan. "I think this is your project. Why don't you begin?"

Rowan blushed, drew in the sand with the toe of her runner, then took a deep breath.

"I guess in a way I did start it." She looked around at the group.

A shadow flitted across the group as an eagle majestically circled over the beach. The eagle opened its beak and gave a wavering cry. The humans watched its silhouette against the bright sky.

The Girl smiled, took a deep breath, and straightened her shoulders. With a sigh like the breeze, the island relaxed.

The eagle circled once more, then soared into the distance.

Watching the eagle had given Rowan a much needed minute to marshal her thoughts. She glanced around the circle again and began.

"It all started when I visited the island last week and saw the little cabin in the centre. You see I've always had this dream...."

Rowan told her story vividly and there were several sighs when she described the death of the baby otter.

"I made research notes and took photos, then Katrina came and confirmed they *are* sea otters, which makes all this pretty special." Rowan paused and gestured around at the bay.

"In the meantime," she continued with a catch in her throat, "Mr. Symchuk discovered he needed to sell the island." She looked across at him. "I guess it's your turn now."

Mr. Symchuk groaned. "Look, I don't want to sell but as some of you already know, I have no choice." He looked unhappily across the beach and out to the kelp beds.

"When I was young, this island was my place of escape, my dream island. As I got older I've enjoyed sharing it with like-minded people, like the Jenners. I wanted to give it to my grandchildren for the same reason, so they

had the chance to own an unspoilt corner of the earth."
He stopped and cleared his throat.

"Thank you for sharing it with us," said Darcy softly.
She slipped her hand into the old man's. "It's been a
wonderful gift, so your dream wasn't wasted."

Mr. Symchuck sighed. "Circumstances have changed
and I've had to put the island up for sale. But we all need
to recognize that whoever buys it is going to develop it."

Mr. Symchuk fumbled in his pocket and passed
Jaimie's photo over to the realtor and gestured to him to
pass it to the Chans.

"You see, most of you here are concerned about the
otters. I have to be concerned about Jaimie." Simply and
straightforwardly he told Jaimie's story.

There was a long silence when he finished.

"I'm really sorry we called in the ITV news team," said
Pat. "We didn't understand."

Martin agreed. "We just thought you were being mean."

Mike Newman gasped. "You mean that helicopter was
the ITV news?"

The Jenner family nodded.

Mike Newman groaned and looked across at Mr.
Symchuk. "Your chances of selling now are zip." He made
a vivid gesture, pulling his hand across his throat. "As soon
as people hear about the sea otters there will be an uproar.
You'd better get ourself a good lawyer. Once the
environmentalists get going there'll be a real mess."

Bevan raised his hand. "Not necessarily. Sea otters
need ocean, a protected marine area. The land is not
important to them. I did some legal research and I think
the sea otters come under the marine protection act, not

the land laws. Maybe it's possible for a land sale to go through with just the water and shore around the bay and headland protected."

The realtor shook his head. "Forget it, environmental arguments could go on for years. The only people who'll get rich from this deal are the lawyers."

Katrina Vasey raised her hand.

"May I?" she asked diffidently.

Everyone nodded.

"I'm a wildlife biologist." She glanced at Mike Newman. "An environmentalist if you prefer. I'd already heard about the sea otters before I met the Jenners, so this situation would have arisen anyway. I'd like to tell you why they are so special, but it would be nice to show you them first."

"Great idea." Grant jumped up and stretched. "Let's all walk up to the headland."

Eagerly the group headed uphill with Hoy and Mr. Chan bringing up the rear. They were intently speaking Chinese in lowered voices and looking very serious.

Rowan led the way. There were the otters. Several were playing in the kelp, while two were floating and grooming.

"Picture perfect," murmured Katrina as she and Mr. Chan took photo after photo.

"A wonderful sight," agreed Mr. Chan.

"Do you know how long it's been since sea otters were last seen in this area?

"Over a hundred years?" ventured Pat.

Katrina nodded. "Let me tell you their story."

Mr. Symchuck and Mr. Chan settled on a fallen tree and

everyone else sprawled on the moss-covered ground.

"For hundreds of years, sea otters were numerous up and down this coastline from Alaska to California. But in the eighteenth century Chinese nobles, Mandarins, bought some pelts from English seamen." Katrina looked across at Mr. Chan.

Mr. Chan nodded. "Sea otter pelts were greatly prized in China," he said. "The fur was so thick and soft that Mandarins paid fabulous prices to have robes made out of them."

Katrina agreed. "So did Russian aristocrats. The upshot was that traders realized they could make fortunes from the sea otters. Fur traders mounted a series of major expeditions that became get-rich killing sprees, and decimated the entire population. The sea otters were easy to kill. In those days the sea otters used the land occasionally and they were curious, unused to humans and friendly by nature. There are stories of them coming up to the hunters and rubbing their heads against the hunter's legs prior to being clubbed."

"Yuck," said Martin quietly.

"At the height of the trade, almost eight hundred sea otters a week were being killed in San Francisco Bay alone. The bodies laid along the beaches were described as a velvet carpet."

The horrors of the story contrasted sharply with the idyllic scene below, of the small group of otters snoozing peacefully while gently rocking up and down on the ocean swell.

"This soon wiped out the entire population, and in 1910, only twenty-four otter pelts were taken, and so few otters seen along the entire coast it was decided they weren't worth hunting any more. They had vanished. In a few short years humans had made a plentiful population almost extinct."

Katrina spread her arm and gestured. "This island must have witnessed some of the massacres."

A shiver of breeze lightly brushed the listeners.

"The other thing that happened," continued Katrina, "is that the otters were very intelligent and soon learned that land was unsafe, and they were safer on sea. In a very few years they evolved to spend their whole life at sea using the kelp beds as 'home.' Unfortunately they have only managed to survive in small pockets ever since. Currently there is a growing population in Monterey Bay and around Big Sur in California, and some stable populations at the north end of Vancouver Island, at Checleset Bay and Bajo Reef."

Katrina looked at everyone with sheer joy on her face. "But this little group... it's the first time there has been any spread this far from the northern group. It's really special and it's going to generate a lot of interest."

The realtor groaned.

Katrina turned to Mike Newman. "These otters can't just go somewhere else. They have to find a healthy well-established kelp bed, and even then the small groups seem to be very vulnerable. Even left alone this group may have trouble growing and surviving."

"And now, please, I think it's my turn." The quiet voice was a surprise to everyone. The family and Mr. Symchuk had almost forgotten about the other strangers within their circle. All eyes turned to Hoy's father.

"As you know, I am a successful businessman. I live part of the year in Hong Kong and part of the year in Vancouver. I have business interests in both countries. Canada has been good to me and also to my son."

Hoy nodded his agreement.

"Some of you have been to Hong Kong," said Mr. Chan looking over at Rowan. "It is a vibrant city teeming with people."

Rowan and Hoy exchanged smiles, remembering the bustling streets and the thousands of people jostling for room with buses, cars, rickshaws, and bicycles.

"Vancouver is also a bustling city," continued Mr. Chan. "In these two cities I spend my days." He paused. "But I too have dreams. A dream of a small unspoilt part of the world that I could escape to now and again."

"Well sir, I think you've found it," the real estate man interjected. "Forget about the hotel. You could build a wonderful home here."

Mr. Chan raised a hand to silence him. "I think you misunderstand me, Mr. Newman. I'd like to own a relatively unspoilt piece of the world, where I can witness nature's harmony."

Rowan again felt herself holding her breath.

Mr. Chan smiled at the real estate man. "You can relax, Mike. If we can all come to some compromises you've made a sale." He then turned to Mr. Symchuk.

"I would like to buy your island sir, but not to turn it into a resort, but as a place to enjoy nature. Not just for me but for others who would like to see the wildlife—including the sea otters—without disturbing them. An ecological centre I think you call it."

Cheers erupted around him, but once more he held up his hand.

"No," he smiled, "I am not a saint; I am a business man. If we do this right, with a special foundation or some permits, I may get big tax concessions from your government, and the chance to make money from ecotourism."

The adults burst out laughing.

Katrina wiped the smile off her face and tried to look serious. "It might not be quite as easy as that, sir. It could take months of negotiations."

"Well, Mr. Symchuk, how about you and I go out for dinner to start negotiations?"

Mr. Chan then turned to Mike Newman. "Mike, check out zoning. See if it's possible to subdivide the island and keep the headland area as a preserve or park and do modest development on the rest. Something along the lines of a small eco lodge or nature centre."

Mr. Chan, and Mr. Symchuk began to walk back to the beach with Mr. Newman flapping along behind them.

Rowan whispered something in Katrina's ear.

Katrina nodded and ran with her camera. "Mr. Chan, Mr. Symchuck, wait!"

The two men turned, smiling.

CLICK! Katrina caught them on film.

"We need to send an update to the news people," Rowan explained.

"Yes, that photo should help keep everyone off your back Mr. Symchuck," agreed Katrina, "especially if we can tell them to phone you. Mr. Chan?"

"Certainly. I can use the publicity!" Mr. Chan smiled

The breeze was freshening. Katrina and Vikki prepared to sail back after making arrangements to keep in touch with Rowan and the Jenners.

"Come over to the paper after work," suggested Vikki to Darcy. "You can help me with the story."

"One thing about it," Darcy remarked. "Rowan's got herself, and everyone else, a project. Look's like we're all going to be involved for months."

"I hope so," said Hoy with a quick smile.

Rowan felt a rush of elation. Working towards making a marine preserve for the sea otters was something she really could sink her teeth into. Her small project had become enormous. Something serious with lasting consequences, and something to make the time fly until her parents' return.

The wind of change blew stronger, and the ebbing tide made fresh patterns in the sand. The breeze ruffled the waves and swirled across the expanding beach. New patterns and configurations appeared and disappeared with every gust. Each person had unknowingly added ripples to the cycle of life. The island watched as the ripples expanded endlessly beyond the horizon. A new dance was beginning.

Acknowledgements

This book would not have come to fruition without help from the Albert Foundation for Literary Arts, Canada Council, the staff of the Vancouver Aquarium, Joy and Teresa at Beach Holme Publishing, Fenella Bazin, and my partner Dave Spalding. Many thanks to everyone.

The song excerpt in Chapter Eight is Mona Douglas' translation of a Manx Gaelic folksong, "Arrane Saveenagh", used by permission of the Manx Heritage Foundation.